THE BOSTONS

THE BOSTONS

Carolyn Cooke

A MARINER ORIGINAL
Houghton Mifflin Company
Boston · New York
2001

Copyright © 2001 by Carolyn Cooke
All rights reserved

For information about permission to reproduce selections from this book, write to Permissions, Houghton Mifflin Company, 215 Park Avenue South, New York, New York 10003.

Visit our Web site: www.houghtonmifflinbooks.com.

Library of Congress Cataloging-in-Publication Data
Cooke, Carolyn, date.
The Bostons / Carolyn Cooke.
p. cm.
"A Mariner Original"
Contents: Bob Darling—Dirt-eaters—The Bostons—Black book—The trouble with money—The sugar-tit—Twa corbies—Girl of their dreams—Mourning party.
ISBN 0-618-01768-2
I. Title.
PS3553.055495 B67 2001
813'.6—dc21 00-046541

Printed in the United States of America

Book design by Robert Overholtzer

QUM 10 9 8 7 6 5 4 3 2 1

Stories from *The Bostons* have appeared in the following publications: "Bob Darling" in *The Paris Review* and in *The Best American Short Stories 1997;* "Dirt-Eaters" in *New England Review* and in *Prize Stories 1998: The O. Henry Awards;* "The Bostons" in *New England Review;* "Black Book" in *New York Stories;* "The Sugar-Tit" in *Agni Review;* and "Twa Corbies" in *The Gettysburg Review* and in *Prize Stories 1997: The O. Henry Awards.* An earlier version of "Girl of Their Dreams," called "Fishing Camp," appeared in *Puckerbrush Review.* "Mourning Party" appeared in *Ploughshares.*

The author is grateful to the National Endowment for the Arts, the Corporation of Yaddo, the Dorland Mountain Colony and the Djerassi Foundation for their encouragement and support.

The stories in *The Bostons* are works of fiction. Names, characters, and incidents are products of the author's imagination or are used fictitiously, and any resemblance to actual persons or events is entirely coincidental.

For Dorothy Cooke and Eleanor Eaton
And for Randall Babtkis, with love

CONTENTS

Bob Darling

BOB DARLING SPENT THE DAY and the evening on the fastest train in Europe. At first the train lugged slowly through yellow towns, then it began to pull together its force and go. The landscape slid past. In one stroke the train braced and broke through the air into a river of dinning sound. It climaxed at 380 kmh. Darling heard this news from a German across the aisle, but he'd already sensed the speed in a deeper bone. His body was attuned to the subtle flux of high speed, the jazz pulse, the fizz.

He closed his eyes, registered the scrape of the antimacassar against his brittle hairs, and dozed. Dying tired him, so did the drugs he took to keep from urinating on the seat. But he never let himself go that far, to close his eyes, unless the buzz of speed was in him, the drone of engines, the *zhzhzh* of jets.

On the seat beside him lounged a beautiful young woman named Carla. She was a baby, vague on facts and ahistorical; she talked too much, she pouted when she didn't get her way, she disliked opera, and she drank. But she had not given him too many terrible disappointments, and overall Darling felt they had been compatible. Paris, coming up, would be the last leg of their trip. Darling planned the Tuileries, the Orangerie, an afternoon at the Louvre, couscous in the Latin Quarter, two nights at the Hôtel Angleterre.

That would be the end of it. Back home he would see her occasionally in the cafés he had first shown her and they would exchange shrill pleasantries. Sometime, perhaps, in the future, he could take her out for dinner and liquor at one of those subterranean French restaurants in Cambridge and afterward press himself on her. But one day she would move, get a job, find a lover, change her life. She would look at her calendar and think she had not seen him in months, or years. But she wouldn't call him until she was sure that he was dead.

(What would that be like? What if he didn't know, if the end of it was not-knowing, if not-knowing was the surprise? What if there was nothing afterward? Where would the information go he had put into his head over the years—the names of kings, the taste of food, the memory of his mother and his father, the fact that *louvre* is early French for "leper," that lava is mainly water, loose facts, what Thoreau said: "Our molting season, like that of fowls, must be a crisis in our lives," the names of women, the names of small hotels? Would the contents of his busy head be wasted, lost?)

He opened his eyes. A crowd of old men on bicycles crashed by outside the window and were gone. Carla leaned into the Michelin guide; the lemony point of her nose and the book vibrated perceptibly to the motion of the train. Her eyes were puffy, from sleep maybe. She still had on her dress from the evening before—a strapless—and some cosmetic residue sparkled on her neck. Her sharp perfume hung on the air. She could sit for hours that way, a packet of French cigarettes and a bottle of Perrier balanced on the seat beside her, her bare feet crossed in her lap. She read any trash for hours and ignored the view. Travel, Darling thought irritably, was a vacation for her.

"The Train à Grande Vitesse," she said now, out of nowhere.

"The TGV, yes, that's the train we're on now," he said.

"You called it the Très Grande Vitesse," said Carla, looking up at him, frowning. "Actually it's the Train à Grande Vitesse—*train*, not *très*."

"That's what they call it informally, I guess," he said, looking across Carla's lap at the blur of France. "Very Great Speed."

"Informally they call it the TGV. And I know what *très* means, thank you."

She was a little bantam, round face, skinny as a refugee, knees like knuckles. Long arms, down to her knees. Twenty, twenty-two. He was not an old man, Darling, but compared to her. In her eyes. From that first afternoon he thought he could get her into bed if he remembered to call her Carla, *not* Paula.

He had found her, funnily enough, unconscious on the T. There were two girls almost exactly alike. It was late afternoon, still hot; the strings of their bathing suits dangled down the backs of their necks, one suit red-checked, the other pale blue. Darling had his leather jacket with him in spite of the heat; he felt a constant chill.

The girls hung from the hand straps, limp as fringe. First, one collapsed. The shoes of interested citizens chattered like sets of teeth around the head. Then the second girl dropped, straight as a rope. They lay there on the floor of the car, completely vulnerable. But two girls fainting stank of conspiracy. No one besides Bob Darling wanted to be taken in.

He hiked his pants so they would not be damaged by his knees and squatted to greet the girls when they woke. The first one opened her eyes, and he saw a flattening out of her pupils, her vision narrowing to familiar and unimaginative suspicions. "What did I, pass out?" she said.

"You seemed to fall," Darling said.

The girl blinked at him. "My wallet still here?" Her hands flew up into the air, then lit on a leather pouch fastened at her waist. "Miracle," she said.

"You want air," he said, and stood her up.

She shook her head. "I've got to go to work." It was a shame, Darling thought; the first girl had a little more shape to her.

"What do you do? I mean that respectfully," Darling assured her, because he thought she might be a dancer, and Paula had been the most marvelously uninhibited dancer. His response to her dancing had always been sexual, but in the most respectful sense.

"Medical records," said the girl.

The second girl opened her eyes and he looked away from the first girl into her face. She was a scrapper, but not bad-looking.

The first girl got off at Charles Street. Darling marveled at how she woke from a dead faint and bussed the other girl's cheeks, then went off to record the claims of a swollen humanity to life and health. Sand still sparkling on the back of her neck. That pale blue string.

His prize was the second girl, Carla; she let him hold her birdy arm. He liked to think he knew the why and the how of the city. Did she know the Such-and-Such Café? The apple cake was the thing to eat. Did she like apple cake? He guided her down into the café, an empty room underground where all the waiters rushed toward him.

But Carla didn't want apple cake. She said she was bored without drinks. She sat across a round table, behind a tumbler of booze.

She would not be shocked by the news of his death, or the idea of his illness. "Things break down," she would think with a shrug. But Darling was still young enough—and the news was fresh enough—that it came to him as a shock, a surprise. Barely two hours before he found her, his doctor and old ally, Carnevali, had sighed deeply and told Darling,

The game
Is not
Quite up
But make your plan.

Appalled, Darling buttoned down his shirt, top to bottom, over his heart, his lungs, his appendicitis scar. Though the day was warm, he put on his leather jacket. He was about to hail a taxi when suddenly he wanted to live among as many people as possible. His eyes flailed like arms, grasping at the grays and browns and bricks of the little Puritan city. He went underground, and waited for the Red Line.

His apple cake lay in crumbs before him on a plate. "Let me show you something," he said, throwing out a spark of spit. He removed a black leather book and a fountain pen from inside his jacket pocket. A lozenge flew out too and rolled under the table. He leaned over the book, showing it to her. "This is Ned Blodgett," he said, and pointed to a list of numbers. "First-rate lawyer." He looked at Carla. "This is his office, this is home—his wife's name is Paula, you'll like her, she's very uninhibited. This is their number in Truro. Ned can get a message to me anytime. Now here is Jane Purbeck, she walks my dog when I'm away—you can call her. This is Jack Shortall, here's his number. These are *reliable people,*" he said.

He closed the book and slid it across the table. "You take it. I know all these numbers." Her hand flickered on the table. "Please," he said. "Even if you don't *want* to leave a message, I will know you *can* leave a message."

"See your pen?" she said. He handed it over. She opened the address book to a blank page near the *W*s and rolled the pen across it experimentally. Then she drew an outline of the couple at the next table, and the table, and a vase with a few flowers in it.

Darling jiggled his leg. "You're an artist," he told her.

"Nope."

He watched her bear down on the nib and smiled, sipped his coffee. "That's a hundred-year-old pen," he said.

Her face emptied. She slipped the cap on the pen and laid it on the table.

"No," he said gently. "Take it—use it."

"Thanks," she said.

Darling scraped his chair on the floor, hobbled it toward her, and told her his name. "You can call me Bob, or you can call me Darling. I mean that respectfully. People call me Darling. Not just women. Men."

"Darling," she said. "Like the girl in *Peter Pan*."

"What? *Peter Pan*?" Darling said excitedly.

"The girl's name—the one who goes to Never-Never Land with Peter."

"Not Mary Martin?"

"No—I meant—the Disney," she said.

Darling sniffed. "Life is too short to talk about Walter Disney," he said.

"Fine," she said. She picked up his pen and twirled it in her fingers.

It was their first *frisson.* Darling savored it with coffee. Together they watched the couple she had drawn eat chicken. The man ate delicately, pulling the underdone meat away from the bone with the point of his knife and actually feeding himself with the blade. His thin white shirt strained to girdle him, and through the fabric the white loops of his undershirt were legible. The woman ate quickly, as if other duties called her. She wore a transparent blouse, which magnified her white arms and the vastness of her brassiere. Once she stopped chewing, she looked up at him and said something. The man didn't look at her, but barked out a laugh. "I'm not feeling flush tonight," he said.

They buttered their bread and rolled it up so more fit into their mouths in one bite. When all the food was gone they wiped their lips with napkins and waited with all their attention until the waiter came and cleared the plates away.

When the waiter came back with pie and coffee on a tray their hands flew up to make room for the dishes, their fingers like birds' wings. They took turns using the cream and sugar. The woman stirred her coffee and smiled. "Everything I've dreamed of for forty years, it's coming true," she said loudly.

Darling squeezed Carla's hand. "Are you hungry?" he asked.

"Oh God, no," she said. "I never eat at night."

*

And yet—he felt this was somehow a contradiction, about eating—she lived above a busy Indian restaurant in Central Square, in one room of Chinese paper lanterns, museum posters and a futon on the floor battened down with sheets and a quilt and ropes of lingerie and clothes. They sat on the futon—it was the only furniture. There was an old coal fireplace with a flue out one side, but the blue rug ran into it. She served him a glass of yellow wine, a ripe tomato. Everything she had, she offered.

She played Stravinsky's *Firebird* on her boom box and rolled pink lipstick over her lips. When she sprang the checkered brassiere of her bathing suit and called him to her bed, he realized he was already there. The slug of strong sensations—desire, hope, *virility*—brought tears to his eyes, which Carla mistook for gratitude.

He hoped to keep his bag of sensations light. Only the most intense sensations interested him. He had looked forward to this train because it was the fastest train. He had been very clear with Carla about this from the start. He wanted to ride the fastest train in Europe. That was one. Two was, he wanted them to eat the wonderful six-course dinner they served on the train. He asked her all about it before they left town, while they were still in the planning stages.

"Fine, Bob, whatever," Carla said when he asked.

Some afternoons they sat under a sun umbrella at the Such-and-Such Café. Darling spread out the map like a tablecloth under their cups and crumbs and napkins and brought out sheets of onionskin encoded with train routes and the names and telephone numbers and addresses of hotels which he tapped out palely on his manual, having forgone the pleasures of his pen. Carla gradually warmed to the idea of the trip. She brushed his cake crumbs from the countries on the map.

She had never heard of Père-Lachaise. She knew only vaguely of Jim Morrison. Her ignorance was vast, ecumenical. He drew on the paper cloth with a yellow pencil. He sketched dreamily, from memory.

"What's that?" she asked.

"It's a baguette, a kind of long French bread."

"I know what a *baguette* is, for God's sake, Bob."

But he could never predict what she knew. He was impressed, for example, by her seamless demand for *caffè macchiato.* But she shrugged and said she didn't know what it meant—she just liked bitter coffee. He wondered whether she had broken his pen, bearing down on the nib, or sold it. He would have liked to show her how the ink went in so that if the pen stopped working she would not worry that she was to blame. His heart ached, imagining her humiliation and shy gratitude.

"You have to speak up—it won't be any good unless we do things you want to do," he told her. "We have to plan everything together. You have to tell me where you want to go, what you want to see."

Carla had never been to Europe. "I don't know," she said.

But I know! I know! Her white dress was ancient to a charming transparency. He would take her—he would show her.

He had read that the dinners on the train were sometimes oversubscribed. You could eat a *croque monsieur* in the bar car, but the thing to do was to get the dinner on the train.

"Fine, whatever," Carla said. "I don't care what I eat."

He leaned across the table, angry, closed his fingers around Carla's wrist, and squeezed.

She ripped his fingers apart, a smooth strong gesture

which surprised him. She laid her hands on her lap. "I eat anything. Scraps," she said.

He sat up late that night at home, walled in by forty years' worth of Michelin guides, tax returns, *Boston Globe*s, *Playbill*s, Symphony programs, creased hotel brochures. He called her at two o'clock in the morning. "Do you want to go to the Sabine Hills or the Villa d'Este at Tivoli? Tell me what you want to do."

There was a pause on the line, a certain flattening out in the expectant air. "Who is this, please?" she said.

And yet, in Europe, it turned out Carla had a terrible talent for knowing exactly what she wanted to do. Right away, in Venice, she saw the Lido from a speedboat. "What is it?" she said, and he told her.

"Oh, I want to go and spend a day," she said.

The next morning she brought it up again—she wanted to go to the Lido and rent a beach chair. But she had agreed already, he reminded her, buttoning his shirt, to walk with him through the Collezione Peggy Guggenheim, and to take a vaporetto to the cathedral at Torcello. Anyway, the last time he had been to the Lido the water was full of white fuzzballs and nobody could swim.

"But I just want to be there," she told him. She jumped up and down on the bed, then jumped off and ran to the window, and pulled back the heavy curtain.

"I thought we could sit in the Piazza San Marco and eat some calamari," he said.

"I don't want to eat!" Carla said. "I could just go out on the boat taxi and meet you later."

They stood barefoot on the rug, facing each other across the unmade bed.

"If that's what you would like to do," he said.

"It is, it is," she said.

And it was done.

He spent the day moving through the crowds at the Piazza San Marco, sliding in a vaporetto through the viscous water to the mudflats, tramping across the Bridge of Sighs. Always water swelled under him in undulating, filthy blackness. He smelled his own sweat through the leather jacket and tasted in his mouth the temperature of his boiling insides. After lunch in a trattoria in Dorsoduro he went out in the air and coughed two drops of blood onto a Kleenex. Embarrassed, he folded the Kleenex into the pocket of his leather jacket and went on to the Piazza, where he threw the Kleenex away.

Hours later he opened the door to his room with his key. The heavy air around Carla was like a fog, an Oriental smokiness. She sat straddled across the bidet wearing just the top of the bikini she had bought in a hotel souvenir shop at the beginning of their trip. (He had been shocked—impressed! —by that impulsive act. He paid a hotel bill, sliding a card from his wallet, signing his name, while Carla went and came back with the bathing suit to show him, black strings in a paper bag. A woman came up beside them with a valise in one hand and a bottle of mouthwash in the other, having some trouble about her bill, putting the mouthwash down on the cashier's polished desk and raking a hand through her bag, her hair ugly around the neck of her coat, muttering "*Merde, merde* . . ." Darling took Carla's arm, wanting to protect her from this woman, and shepherded her away.)

Carla's skin was burned red around the bathing suit top and she had long scratch marks up and down her back. She turned slowly from the sound of running water to look at him in the doorway. Her chin twisting over her shoulder pulled cords in her neck that opened her mouth. She seemed to be manipulated by strings.

Some bleary look in her eyes got in the way of his concern for her.

He folded his leather jacket over his arm. "I may just meet you downstairs," he said.

Carla rolled her eyes and turned away. He went out, closing the door behind him. He bought a postcard at the front desk and sat down at a narrow table in the lobby.

"Dear Paula," he wrote. "It is now six o'clock Sunday evening. The clock atop the Italian steps has struck those hours with an ancient quality. An array of birds with a multiplicity of sounds is announcing its departure this evening. The light is muted and pink, the city overall is waiting." He read it over—it all seemed beside the point somehow. She had been so direct with him in her postcard from Oslo, the small block letters: "You are an elf, darling. But I am not really interested in elves."

He folded the card over and over itself and slipped it into his pocket just as Carla appeared. She wore her thrift store strapless; she had tied her hair back and pushed tiny pearls into her earlobes. Her skin had a yellow-blue pallor which made her seem unearthly, untouchable—it dazzled him. They had Pellegrino water together, then dinner at a place on one of the canals, pasta first, then calamari in ink and, at Darling's suggestion, two bottles of wine. "How many bottles do we need?" Darling asked Carla. "I mean that respectfully. I want to get drunk too." They drank fast out of tiny green glasses. Bob Darling shouted, "I'm drunk! Pow! Life is a glorious mist!"

He ordered a gondola, then the ancient wood walls began

to close around him. He threw money down on the table. A waiter put his arms around Carla's waist and lifted her into the gondola. Darling's vision closed down on her dress, which seemed to have no front or back. Someone handed him a plate of cake, and then Carla's hand. He held them both; the hand, the cake. Looking out over the black water he pictured the way he would open the world to her, the blown glass choker he would fit around her neck, the lire liquid in his hand, pouring into her. He passed the plate of cake to Carla and gripped the knob of her knee.

"You want to know what the janitor in my building said about you, Darling?"

"If you like," he said.

"You told that terrible joke, remember? She said, 'I don't trust one single thing about that man.'" She squeezed his arm.

On the way out of the gondola she slipped and her leg sank into the inky canal. Walking up the narrow stairs to their room he heard the sucking sound of her shoe. Then she was asleep, painful-looking, sunburned. He tried not to look at her, at the marks on her back. Instead he lay back on his pillow, unable as ever to sleep in silence, and turned pages in the black book he had bought for her to record her trip. "He was his own whole world," she had written. "He wore wool sweaters on hot days, bikini underwear. Every day he sent his pajamas down to be washed—why?—and they came back ironed. He saved anything that had words on it—theater tickets, programs, newspapers, napkins—but he never read anything. He carried a skin change purse that I wanted. He could walk for hours without stopping, but only in the city. He gave out his telephone number to everyone."

Her hand flopped out and lay on his arm. He looked at

her things from the day tossed out like ropes at sea—her bikini bottom, the black dress, the rich cake nearly intact on a plate, the Oriental smell of her perfume, the ether of liquor. He read more, snatches here and there—her block letters were full of effort but difficult to read. "Asked if he could cut me just a little bit on the leg." (His eye shot up, electric, but fell again to the page.) "In an umber room/he kissed my mouth/nibbled my mouth like an ant/carried me away/like crumbs." He let Carla's hand lie on his arm until it felt heavy, then he moved it away.

The argument was about the difference between naked and nude. He started it with her in France, in the countryside, over dinner in a small hotel. His cutlet had a crust on it and swam in a sauce. He would not drink wine from the leaden pitcher.

He pushed his plate away and laid his napkin on the table. "I want to tell you a story about my friend Paula," he said, careful to use Paula's name. "She and her husband lived on Mount Vernon Street—'the most respectable street in America,' Henry James called it—or maybe he said, 'the only respectable street in America.'" Darling paused. "Do you read James?" he asked her gently.

She looked at him.

"You should! You should!"

"Why should I?" she asked, slicing into her cutlet.

"The passion!"

She put down her fork and laughed at him.

"But listen. My friend Paula gave a dinner party on Mount Vernon Street. We drank champagne, we ate terrible food off Italian plates. We are not a bohemian crowd at all, you understand. But suddenly Paula came into the room and unzipped the gown she was wearing and it just fell around her feet like a puddle. I'll never forget it. She was naked, she was statuesque, celebrating, inviting, brave. To say she was *nude* would be an insult."

"What did people do?" Carla asked.

"Of course no one did anything. We were far too respectful. A woman like Paula naked in a room, a grown woman at the height of her power, is almost untouchable."

"Why would she want to be untouchable?" Carla asked.

"You mean, did she want us to see her as an object of art or an object of sex? Isn't that what you mean, you think these things are different?"

Carla sighed. "Poor Paula."

"Poor *Paula*?" He could hear the mockery in his voice. Spit formed in the corner of his mouth.

The word he used was wrong, she argued. You would never say a child was nude—it would be an offense to the child, it would be obscene. Nudity corrupted nakedness with eyes, she said, climbing up onto her high horse, conservative as a child.

Would she prefer the lighter and more moral state? he asked her, mocking. Which was the more "natural" state? If nudity was more artful than nakedness, wasn't it also less natural? So it followed, since she was always interested in being more "natural," that she would rather get naked than nude.

"I'm not interested in being more natural," she said.

He sent his dinner back twice. It was an impossible place. He went upstairs to the loo; through a hole in the floor he saw the top of her head, saw her spear a corner of his cutlet with her fork. The whole hotel swarmed with flies. Standing over the urinal, he thought of how only sauternes could save you from the richness of foie gras. Poor, poor liver! Their room down the hall—she had flung the casement open and let flies in there. But what could it matter? He buttoned up his pants and to hell with it, did not wash his hands.

After dinner she wanted to go for a walk—through the fields of sunflowers. He tried to think of a way to hurt her so she would remember him, but it was hard to walk without seeing his feet, through the wide flower heads that faced and mocked him. His hand attached to her damp shoulder with a sound of suction.

"Your eyes are so cold," she said.

"What did you say?"

"It's you—you're cold!"

He took hold of the other shoulder. He felt a wild urge to bite it.

"Do you think you tricked me? Do you think you're crafty?" she burst out. She pushed him off, away. He fell back stiffly, like an old man, pulling the heavy-headed flowers down with him. The ground sucked him in. He pulled wildly at her arm with his hand, and she recoiled so violently that she brought him upright.

The train reeled north at great speed. Carla opened her eyes, stretched her arms, and yawned. She looked out the window. "What time is it?" she asked.

"Five o'clock," he said. "We have dinner in half an hour."

She sat up now, serious, and rolled orange lipstick over her lips, examining her mouth in a pocket mirror inscribed (from a lover?) "A little bit every day." She closed the mirror and dropped it into one of her shapeless bags. "Oh, I can't eat at five-thirty, can you? Let's go and have a drink in the bar."

It was unbelievable. He could have pulled out her eyes.

"I asked you a month ago about eating dinner on this train," he said.

"I don't like to eat at night," she said.

The train overtook its whistle. All sound now was behind his ears. He had an image of himself in black space, pinned to the back of a rocket. He dropped his arms down like two great weights on the arm rests—to steady himself.

"Please, eat this dinner with me," he said.

"Look," said Carla. "Why can't we just go into the bar car? I can't stand being crammed in here like a sardine. Wouldn't it be more interesting to go and have a drink and look out the windows and talk to people?"

"I don't want to," Darling said. "What I want to do is what we arranged a month ago. I want to eat the dinner they serve on this train. I want to sit right here and eat the dinner they serve on the train!"

"I don't," she said.

"You wanted to a month ago when you said you would," he reminded her.

"Bob, for God's sake, a month ago." She raked her hair with a hand and looked over the tops of the seats at the people all around them, at the oblivious heads.

"Eat dinner with me tonight. Please, Carla, just do," he said.

"Why do you want me to do everything I don't want to do? Why would you want that?" she said. Her eyes went everywhere but to him.

He looked at Carla until she ran out of places to look, until there was nowhere to look but at him. He sat in her path, in the aisle seat. Carla had the window. Her eyes floated over him.

"I don't see the point of asking me to sit here and eat my

dinner on a tray when I'm not hungry and I don't want to."

"Could you do something for me just because I ask you to, or do you think dinner is too much to ask?" he said. He looked at his fingers vibrating in his lap, melded into a warped hideous undifferentiated hand, a paw.

Her eyes were glass. She looked past him.

He hugged his knees to his seat's edge and let her climb over him into the aisle. She stood up and stretched herself out limb by limb like an animal. He looked up and she rolled her green eyes across him.

"I need francs," she said.

He reached into his pocket and pulled out the skin purse she had coveted—so she would know he had read what she wrote. "Take it," he said.

But she gave no sign of remembering. She caressed the skin between her fingers, tears in her eyes. "Look, I'm sorry I've been this big disappointment to you on your trip," she said. "I did my best, OK?"

He looked into her face for any sign—any sign.

"OK?" Carla said again.

"Take a ferryboat to hell!" he shouted.

She walked toward the bar car, against the speed and pull of the train. He saw her fingers move over the skin purse; it was the scrotum of a lamb. A steward brought the entire meal at once—chicken breasts in white sauce, green beans, apple tarts.

He sat quietly, penned into his seat by his tray. He looked across the seat Carla had left and at the tray on the folding table in front of it, and beyond that out of the window at the blur of France. He considered moving into her seat, but the empty seat was part of his view: not-Carla. He tasted his unpromising dinner and discovered that he was hungry, but still discerning.

He ate his dinner slowly, looking carefully across the empty seat at the blur, and at Carla's untouched chicken. All right: it was the fastest train in Europe. The food was above average. Everything was moving. The landscape outside looked as if it were underwater, wet, bleeding green-yellow-blue. He gripped a tray in each hand and in one motion switched his empty tray with hers. He ate the second dinner more quickly than the first, kept the fork gripped in his hand and moved it back and forth between the tray and his mouth until he had to confess he was glad she had left. He scooped up Carla's apple tart, then wiped the ooze from his lips with a napkin, virtuous. He looked at the outside from the inside of the train. There was no comparison between this train and other trains he had ridden. He was like a fish being carried underwater in a current faster than a fish could swim. A cradle of fantastic motion. He let himself go then, and rested, and slept.

Dirt-Eaters

We turned off at the Cheese House, which was round and painted yellow, gouged with black holes. After that, the country seemed real. Horses stood bored behind little fences of chicken wire and lath. The skeletons of gray barns rattled beside long farmhouses painted white and green. Old cars multiplied; so did snowmobiles tilted on the green humps of yards, toy tractors, red bicycles leaning up against red maples, tire swings.

Mum drove. Grand sat wide and ladylike beside her and said wasn't it comical to see reindeer on the roof in June. I looked up and saw a broken plastic Santa Claus hung down behind a metal sleigh instead of commanding it, his black whip broken in two. "Isn't it just like those Burnses to be so lax? Haven't they always been nothing?" Grand said.

There were Burnses everywhere, and they were all bad news. Grand knew about all of them, who the fathers of the children were and the names and the ages of the cousins and aunts, and how they had married each other and made the family even worse.

"Buzz Burns, you mean?" asked Mum.

"He shot his wife!" shouted Grand. "She got him back, though."

"Oh, Mumma. I bet they're saying in there, 'There goes old Maggie—doesn't she come from a great old line?'"

"My grandfather was the son of a duke!" Grand said. The words flew up like hands in front of her face.

"So he told us," Mum said.

Grand clutched her big square purse in her lap like a baby she kept smoothing down. A car passed around us. Mum veered the wheel. "Jesus God, maniacs!" she said.

"Did you bring a bottle?" Grand said.

"I brought a bottle of wine," Mum said.

"Coo, wine!" Grand said.

"They don't have to drink it today," Mum said. "They could put it aside."

"I brought a *bottle*," said Grand.

We rode through a jungle of birches and hackmatack and maple and pine. Aunt Annie and Uncle Owen and all their kids had just moved back from wherever they had been living, and had been camped out at the Dysharts' for two months. The Dysharts had five or six kids. It was supposed to be a picnic.

We drove up alongside the Dysharts', where they kept more cars than people. They all stayed in two toy-looking houses—one house where they ate, with the TV and the stove, and the other house where some of them slept. The first person we saw was Louise in the yard with her dirty-looking horse; her hand on the side of the horse's head reminded me of last time, of the head coming down to take the shucked clams we held out on our palms. Louise was my age, eight. She had pink cheeks and wore a dirty pink dress. She never seemed exasperated by anyone. She waved and ran on toward us, her bare feet kicking up to the backs of her knees.

The Dysharts' other four or five kids and Aunt Annie and Uncle Owen's four kids were running all over the field between the two houses. Aunt Annie and Mrs. Dyshart spilled out the kitchen door. They both had curly hair to their shoulders and pink and white checkered one-piece bathing suits that tied at the backs of their necks. They had red toenails and cut-off blue jeans for shorts, and glasses rattling ice in their hands. Uncle Owen and Louise's father, Mr. Dyshart, walked out behind them, two skinny men dressed in long pants, black shoes and socks, and short-sleeved shirts. They stood in the driveway, holding cigarettes cupped behind their backs.

Mum drove carefully, her knuckles curved over the steering. She slammed on the brakes whenever she saw a person. "Jesus God!" she said. "These kids are *right under* my wheels." Grand ran red lipstick over her lips and kissed a Kleenex. Mum parked the car and jumped out of her side. She had on blue-jean shorts too, but she was still dramatic with her pixie cut and cat's-eye dark glasses and her black T-shirt.

Louise ran up and looked in the window. "Hey—you," she said. "What's your name?"

"I am *Molly,*" I said.

"I forgot. Are you my cousin or are you with them?"

My cousins Ross and Lenny and Trudy were yelling in the yard. I said I was with them. Aunt Annie opened the car door on Grand's side and she and Grand jabbed their cheeks at each other. Grand brought a bottle of Jim Beam out of her purse and snapped the clasp closed again, a rich-sounding sigh and a click. "Oh, Maggie, we were hoping for one of your pies," Uncle Owen joked.

Grand flapped her arms at him, smiled and puckered her lips. "Isn't he comical?" she said. Uncle Owen took the bottle and Grand's arm and hauled her out of the car. Grand's dress spread out when she stood up and shrank up her leg past the knee.

Troy, also my cousin, was the only one of the kids Grand didn't know about. He was already two, and Aunt Annie and Uncle Owen hadn't mentioned him yet because Grand would have had such a fit it would probably have sent her to bed for a year. We all said this, but Grand had gone to bed for a month every time Aunt Annie had another baby, and even if Grand *had* gone to bed for a year because of Troy, she would have been out now.

It was exciting, having Grand not know, wondering when she would add it up. Troy sat on the ground away from the kids on the field, but Grand could have seen him if she tried. His hair hung in white whips on his shoulders and he didn't really play. He never looked up at any of the other kids, just stirred dirt around in a tin cup with a stick. He was small for his age, and had on a pair of overalls all my cousins had worn before. It seemed impossible, even among my running cousins and five or six Dyshart kids on the field, that Grand did not notice Troy now, and see who he was. It made her seem stupid. The adults rolled their eyes at each other while Grand made her way to the kitchen house, busy looking down the two white poles of her legs to her sneakers in the rutty dirt.

The day dragged the way it always did when our family had a picnic. The adults went into the house and my cousins Ross and Lenny and Trudy and I stood around the yard for a long time with our arms hanging down. Cousin Trudy had a dirty doll hanging from her hand by its hair and she didn't remember me either. Troy just sat by himself in the dirt with his stick and his cup, and beyond him the Dyshart kids played a rough game of tag. Except for Louise, the Dysharts' kids were all just names and faces.

"What'd you get for Christmas?" Lenny finally asked me.

"A desk," I said.

"A *desk*? I got about three hundred dollars' worth of tropical fish," he said.

"Where are they now, big shot?" Ross said.

"Shut up," Lenny told Ross.

"I also got a tape recorder," I said, "but it doesn't work."

"Eight track or reel-to-reel?" Ross asked.

"Reel-to-reel," I said.

"You should have gotten an eight-track," Ross said.

"What happened to your fish?" I asked Lenny.

"He ate them, the dumb-ass," Ross said.

"Shut up!" Lenny said.

"I dared him to," said Ross. "That's how dumb he is."

We climbed stairs in the second house, up to the room where the kids lived. It seemed to be made of girls' dresses, blue jeans and red flannel printed with cowboys and Indians, and everything smelled warm of wood and sugar and pee.

"I'm so bored," Ross said. He lit matches and tossed them lighted out the window. We all looked out the window to see if a fire would start.

"We're never going to eat," Lenny said.

"I thought it was a picnic," I said.

"Yeah, right," Ross said. "A *picnic*."

"Did you eat anything before?" Lenny said.

"I had a honey bun at home," I said.

"You're so goddamned rich," Lenny said.

"We'd be rich too if we didn't have so many goddamned kids," Ross said. He held a lighted match in his fingers and closed his mouth around it. When he opened his mouth again the match had gone out.

"All we ever get here is cereal," Lenny said. "Yesterday we didn't even have any milk. Goddamn Annie made us put goddamn water on it."

"Just one day," sneered Ross. "What's the matter, baby, you can't take it?"

"Eat dirt, jerk," Lenny said.

"You all live here now?" I asked.

"Nah, we're just staying here until we move," Lenny said.

"Where are you moving?"

"Maybe Boston. My father's got a guy down there wants him to come do some work for him. You ever hear of Billerica, Massachusetts?"

"No," I said.

"Well, this guy has a house that cost a million bucks in Billerica, Massachusetts. The house is about a mile long. I went in it, too. You want to talk about rich, this guy has a swimming pool in the middle of his house. He's got his own putting green—"

But Ross interrupted. "I'll bet you twenty bucks we don't move to Boston." Lenny just looked at him.

"Do you all sleep in here?" I asked. It looked like twenty kids did. Someone had tried to make a fort out of the clothes and sheets and blankets, which were tied up to chairs and doorknobs and hung over the bare mattresses like tents.

"Yeah," said Ross. "Lenny sleeps over there with the little kids who wet their beds and I sleep with Louise."

"I don't wet."

"You do so wet."

"You don't sleep with Louise."

"I do too sleep with her. Louise lets me ball her," Ross said.

"You lie."

"Molly won't let me ball her, will you, Molly?" Ross said. I shook my head no and looked out the window. He lit a match and held it until it burned down to his finger, then he jerked it out the window and we leaned over the sill together, watching it fall. "I can't wait to get out of this place," he said.

Uncle Owen cooked all day in the kitchen, laying spoons on the stove that bled spaghetti sauce down the oven door. Aunt Annie scrubbed clams with a wooden brush and dropped them live into a pot of water. The kitchen table filled up with ashtrays and glasses and rings on the table, Grand's bottle of Jim Beam, a bottle of coffee brandy and a carton of milk. When we kids ran in Mum said in a sensational voice, "Head for the roundhouse, they can't corner you there!"

Mrs. Dyshart and Aunt Annie seemed to expand in the warm kitchen. They untied their bathing suit strings and tucked them into the bras of their suits, pulled off their earrings and laid them down on the kitchen table. Pins slid from their hair. They played a game with Ross, took turns burning holes with a lighted cigarette in a napkin that held a dime suspended over a water glass. Yellow and blue stained the top of Mrs. Dyshart's brown arm. She and Aunt Annie wore their tans like masks, and they took turns holding the cigarette in the same stiff, careful way, as if the broken red polish on their nails was still wet and fresh. Ross kept taking drags on the cigarette to keep it going until finally Aunt Annie said, "*Ross.*" A fan of white lines unfolded around her brown mouth. She burned another hole in the napkin and the dime clunked into the glass.

"Junkman came and gave me twenty dollars for that alabaster statue I kept on the mantel," Grand said.

Mum's back shot up straight in her chair. "Not the bust of William Shakespeare," she said.

Grand nodded. "That old thing. Dust all over it and some curlicue broke off. Junkman gave me twenty dollars, isn't that rich?"

"Oh, Mumma, I would have given you fifty dollars," Mum said.

"Coo!" said Grand. "Where would you get cash?"

"How could you, Mumma, that bust was part of our family. I remember that bust in Grandma's kitchen at the Blodgetts'. William Shakespeare," Mum said.

"Oh, Lucy, you're so dramatic," Grand said. "I think I paid twenty-five cents for it at the Episcopal church fair. Junkman wanted to look at Grampy's Civil War rifle he bought in Bangor for a dollar, but I couldn't find it."

"I'd sell the gun before the Shakespeare," Mum said.

"I could probably get you a hundred bucks for a Civil War gun," Uncle Owen said.

"Oh, coo," said Grand.

Mum told the old stories about Grand. When Grand was young she had red hair and she was a star forward on the girls' basketball team. They called her "Shimmy" Purton because of the way she danced with boys.

"Isn't that wicked?" Grand asked. "Your fat old Grand dancing the shimmy? My mother Purton used to have a fit."

"Shimmy, shimmy, coconut," Uncle Owen teased Grand, swagging his hips. Grand waved him away, but she bunched her lips at him.

"I remember Grandma Purton's rice pudding," Mum said. "She baked it in that old Clarion oven. It would cook there all afternoon and her kitchen smelled of cinnamon and sugar and the raisins she used, the currants. And when the pudding was done she'd say, 'I shouldn't,' but we always had bowls of it together with cream on top."

"I don't remember that," Aunt Annie said. She slid Mum's

pack of Kents across the table, lit a cigarette with Mum's lighter and blew two or three smoke rings.

"How do you remember that, Lucy? If that isn't comical," Grand said.

"I think my life was more real to me when I was six than it is now," Mum said.

"That's a good one," said my aunt.

Mum told the old story of when Grand was just a little girl and her sister Doris died. Grandma Purton screamed, *Why did this one have to be taken?* The whole house shook, and Grampy Purton had to come and quiet her so the Blodgetts wouldn't hear. And then when they laid Doris out on the kitchen table where they ate, dressed in a new dress that cost thirty dollars, Grand was sitting with her and she saw Mrs. Blodgett coming down the walk to pay her respects. Grand ran and hid under the stairs so Madam wouldn't see her. "Can you imagine?" Mum said.

"Isn't it something how she remembers it so vivid? *I* don't remember it that vivid," Grand said.

Ross reached for Aunt Annie's cigarette but Aunt Annie looked at him without moving her face at all and dropped the cigarette into the glass with the dime. The cigarette smoked in the glass. Aunt Annie opened a magazine and turned the pages with the pads of her fingers.

"I don't think it was terrible," Grand said. "It was what we knew."

"That's Lucy, trying to make a tragedy out of everything," said Uncle Owen.

"It *is* tragic," Mum said.

"Boo hoo, I'm crying," Uncle Owen said.

Mum looked around for someone who would understand her.

Uncle Owen sat down beside me with his drink in a coffee mug. He puckered his lips and made kissing noises. Then he sang:

> Your teeth are yeller
> Who's your feller?
> You some ugly child.

"Why don't you stop moping around and get married, Lucy?" Uncle Owen asked Mum.

"I don't want to take care of a man," Mum said. "I have a kid to take care of. I have dreams of my own, damn it," she yelled, suddenly furious.

"You ought to make a home for someone, have more children. That's what we're here for—family," Uncle Owen said.

"He's crazy!" Grand told Aunt Annie.

"Oh, for God's sake, Owen. I *have* a family. I want . . . a life. Or is a kid a life?" Mum asked as if she thought he really might know, but Uncle Owen wasn't listening.

He leaned close to her. "I remember the first time I saw Molly. I said, 'A baby's a miracle, isn't it? Just imagine this little bundle twelve or thirteen years from now drinking jiz in the back seat of a Ford.' Hey, Lucy?"

Mum threw her glass at him. It bounced off his chin and clunked on the table. "Shut up, you filthy man, you old reptile, you stinker!" Mum yelled. "You didn't hear that, Molly," she told me.

Uncle Owen licked Jim Beam off his chin and the back of his hand, making loud sucking noises. "Oh, Lucy, this is good!" he said.

Mum stood up. "That's it," she said. "Get your things, Mumma, Molly. We're leaving."

I got up to go. Grand stayed where she was, not even paying attention, just looking at Troy, who was sitting on the floor talking to his stick, but not in any voice you could hear. Aunt Annie stood up suddenly and said, "Jesum, Owen, aren't you going to feed these kids?"

Uncle Owen went over to the stove and poured red sauce over plates of spaghetti. Aunt Annie handed around bowls of clams. Grand was looking at Troy without really seeing him, and then her eyes focused and we saw that she had guessed about Troy, had figured it out. "Oh my Lord, you've got another one!" she said.

A line between Grand's eyes and Troy was clear as a rope in the air, tying them together. "You've got another one, haven't you?" Grand shrilled.

"Say hello to your grandson Troy, Mumma," Aunt Annie said. She held out a bowl of clams to Grand, but Grand wouldn't take it. She uncrossed her legs and planted her feet wide apart on the floor. She leaned over her lap toward Troy and really looked at him.

Everybody looked at Grand look at Troy.

"You got another one?" Grand asked again. She heaved up on her feet. Her legs looked like two white flagpoles holding up a nation.

"We have Ross and Lenny and Trudy and Troy," Aunt Annie said.

Uncle Owen suddenly wasn't anywhere—a long brown spoon stuck out of the pot. Grand took a step toward Troy and all the adults jumped on her and held her arms, except Aunt Annie, who was still holding the bowl of clams. Louise put down her plate and picked up Troy and his stick, and walked out the front door.

Grand was just breathing. "You must be crazy," she said to Aunt Annie.

We kids, except for Louise and Troy, sat on the floor with our backs against the kitchen wall, buttering rolls, skimming gray veils off the necks of clams, rolling spaghetti around our forks.

"Oh, Mumma," Mum said. "*Jesus,* Mumma." She picked up her glass from the floor and banged over to the counter for ice, so it was just the Dysharts holding Grand's arms, and Grand leaning toward Aunt Annie now, hissing at her, but not really trying to break away.

"You must be crazy," Grand said, spitting a little toward Aunt Annie. "I'd think you'd be ashamed!"

"I am not ashamed," Aunt Annie said. She put down the plate of food and sat at the table, but instead of eating she lit another cigarette. Facing Grand, Aunt Annie sat there, her wide brown chest puffed out from the top of her bathing suit, blowing the smoke away from Grand's eyes and smoking with one elbow raised in the air the way Grand herself did it.

The spaghetti tasted delicious, hard and then soft against your teeth, and the soft bellies of the clams tasted gray and grainy from the tiny pearls of sand they had eaten.

Grand, who hadn't known about Troy for two years, didn't notice he was gone.

"I'm not going to say hello to it," Grand said.

"Troy almost died of a hole in the stomach when he was three months old," Aunt Annie told Grand. White lines fanned out at the corners of her red watering eyes.

"Why didn't you get yourself fixed when I gave you the money?"

"I used the money to pay for Troy's operation, Mumma," Aunt Annie said.

*

After the picnic we left our plates and bowls on the kitchen counter and climbed back to the kids' room with our hands full of Oreos. We talked about who was wanted and who wasn't, scraping off the white frost of sugar between the cookies with our front teeth. All of Aunt Annie and Uncle Owen's kids were mistakes, especially Troy. But I had been planned and wanted.

"Yeah, *right,*" Ross said, his gums black with cookie.

All of the Dyshart kids were surprises but were wanted, so Louise claimed.

Inside the house ice cracked and broke. Grand yelled, "I could shoot that man!" Mum and Aunt Annie yelled back at her, but Grand's voice soared up over them and hung in the yard: "If I had a gun, I'd shoot him!"

Louise, the thrill of violence lighting her eyes, kneeled down around Troy and told him that Grand would shoot him if she found him. She pulled him close and in a rough motherly way explained over and over that it was his fault Grand was mad and she would shoot him with a gun unless he did exactly as we said. Troy didn't say he understood—he babbled to his stick. He stood still while we wrapped him and his stick in a red blanket printed with cowboys and Indians. Then we hid him in a trunk—closed him up with some toys and old sneakers. We built a maze around him, so if Grand were to come up with a gun she would have to crawl between chairs covered with snow jackets and Louise's dresses.

We went outside to keep watch for Grand, but right away we were bored. Louise took me to the paddock where her horse stood in the muck out front of his stall looking at us with cloudy eyes. He was old, or maybe he was sick. His head hung close to the ground.

Louise didn't have a saddle—I didn't know if she could ride the horse or not, whether the horse could see well enough to be ridden or run. Crossing the paddock was like walking through glazed snow, any minute your foot could crack through the dry manure and sink down. We crossed over and rubbed the horse's long head and talked to it as if it were a baby. Louise still had on her dirty pink dress. She pulled out an extra pair of hip boots for me to put on over my shorts and sneakers. Together we mucked out the stable with shovels and swung the black piles over the fence and laid down new hay. Boots, shovels, everything was in the little stable that we needed.

The sun flattened and turned orange, the trees turned black, the crickets rubbed their wings. We heard Grand's voice coming out of the kitchen, yelling something tearful. Mum yelled back in a hard voice, "*Mumma.*"

Louise and I peeled off the rubber boots and left them fallen on the ground like legs. We thumped up the stairs of the second house. All the other kids had gone out to the old pickup in the field to play chicken. Louise and I crawled through the maze of clothes and chairs, opened the trunk and unwrapped Troy. At first we thought he was dead—he was so pale and a vein showed blue on his forehead. We pulled him from the trunk and laid him out on the floor. Right away he opened his eyes and vomited his dinner. Louise kneeled beside him and wiped his mouth with clothes. We were still playing, but it felt serious and real.

She cleaned Troy and dressed him in footed pajamas, then picked him up. He was long and heavy, like a monkey in her arms. We walked across the yard to the kitchen where she dropped him in Aunt Annie's lap. Grand didn't seem upset by the sight of Troy anymore. He was just another one.

Mum said it was time to go. Troy sat up and rubbed his eyes. We all went outside where it was suddenly the time of night when mosquitoes buzzed and bit, and blue bats orbited the yard. "Look at the bats!" Mum said, and we all looked up, except for Grand, who screamed and covered her hair with her hands. Then Ross and Lenny ran over and asked Mum, "Please, Aunt Lucy. Do Bette Davis."

Mum tapped a Kent out of her pack and lit it with her Bic. She puffed out a few clouds of smoke, raised her chin so the cords in her neck showed and waved her arm toward Uncle Owen's car at the other end of the yard. Uncle Owen was sitting in the driver's seat, not going anywhere. The little light from the ceiling glowed down on him.

Mum turned into Bette Davis, a smoking killer. "You want to speak to my husband? He's in there," she said, waving to Uncle Owen. "But you can't speak to him. You see, I've just killed him," Mum said. She puffed more on her cigarette and let go of Bette Davis slowly. For a second she was both Bette Davis and Mum, then finally she dropped her chin and her face softened into the usual worry lines on her forehead, and she was just Mum.

Mr. Dyshart took his cigarette from the cup of his hand and stuck it in his mouth while he clapped.

Aunt Annie said, "Isn't she something?" and tapped her palms together in silent, useless applause.

Uncle Owen still sat in his broken car on the other side of the yard, slumped down so all you could see was the top of his head and the coffee mug on the dashboard and the yellow bulb glow.

Mum stuffed her cigarettes and her lighter in the pockets of her cutoffs.

"You're such a card," Ross told Mum.

"OK, Molly, you work the pedals and I'll steer," Mum said, her old drunk joke. But Grand had already buckled herself in up front. I climbed in back and put my seat belt on. Aunt Annie and Mr. and Mrs. Dyshart turned toward the kitchen and Aunt Annie saw Troy squatting near the front door in his footed pajamas holding a tin cup full of what looked like rocks and dirt. "Oh, Jesum *Crow,* he's eating dirt again. Look at you, you little dirt-eater," she said, swatting the cup out of his hand. It rattled across the rutty yard. Troy's head hung sideways and he looked up at his mother with one eye and showed a row of small square teeth. It was his smile.

"Come on," Aunt Annie said, and yanked him up with one hand, and they all walked back into the kitchen. Mr. Dyshart closed the door behind them.

Grand whimpered in front. She opened the big purse on her lap and pulled out a Kleenex. Then in slow thumps she began to take off her blazer. Mum reached over to help peel the sleeves back from her shoulders and the car pitched from one side of the road to the other.

"I'm so moist," Grand complained.

"Jesus, Mumma, you could at least have taken the jacket off. We're *family.*"

"My arms are fat," Grand said.

Mum drove past the broken, hanging Santa Claus on the Burnses' roof. "They're just as bad as those Burnses, all those kids and *nothing*!" Grand said, and blew her nose. "We Purtons weren't much. But we were something."

"Your legs still look nice, Mumma," Mum said. "This afternoon I was noticing your calves."

"You think so?" Grand said, dabbing her Kleenex at the end of her nose.

"Your calves are very shapely for a woman your age."

"Troy thought you were going to shoot him, Grand," I said.

Grand and Mum both spun their heads around. Mum recovered and looked back at the road. "What?" she said, the *t* rattling out behind the word.

"She thought I wanted to shoot that baby," Grand said. "My Lord!"

"Grand isn't going to shoot anybody, you got that?" Mum said.

"She thought I wanted to shoot the baby!" Grand said again. She wiped her eyes with the Kleenex. "What must you think of your Granny."

We drove a while without talking.

"Owen was using that old coffee mug," Mum said to Grand. "No wonder he has diverticulitis. What that man drinks. Gee, God."

"That's an alcoholic, drinking out of a coffee mug," Grand agreed.

Mum smiled tightly at the Cheese House as we came up to the turn.

"What on earth is that building over there?" Grand asked, pointing at it, her finger bent against the window glass. "When did they put that up? That used to be the Vermeer farm."

"That's the Cheese House, it's been there forever, Grand," I said.

"It's round, is it?" said Grand. She didn't trust herself. "I never saw it."

"You need to use your eyes, Mumma," Mum said.

But Grand wasn't looking. Her finger slid down the glass. "A house shaped like a cheese," she said. "Isn't that comical."

The Bostons

I DON'T CARE if you're Pablo Picasso, I won't live in a museum!" said Martha Sargent. "Who's going to look at two hundred pictures of the State House? Ruth isn't interested and neither are the grandkids. Look at you, making new ones!"

Mr. Sargent sat on a straight-backed chair at the breakfast table, painting in a sketch of the dome. The glittering bulb, vivid! round! Seen and drawn "through a window"—the triumph of Bulfinch. He dipped his brush in the glass of water on the table as his wife, whose head was just visible behind the large brown box in her arms, passed him on her way to the door. "Stop *painting,*" she begged him. "Get out of the habit of putting everything down. Keep it in your head, up here." She took one arm from around the box and rapped her knuckles on her head.

His head? It sloshed, it ached with age. His hand was the opening, the lip of the pitcher; out poured the figures he saw, though the world remained shadowy and incomprehensible.

Martha Sargent, however, judged hard. *I prefer the yellowy one,* she might remark of his *Sunset on the Mall. That gray one* (dawn view) *is so gloomy.* Now she had no patience for clutter, but Mr. Sargent stood firm. What eyes could he see through but his own? She herself had dipped a brush at one time; she had an exaggerated sense of perspective, which was, he felt, probably unintentional. When he first knew her she used to go out in all weather with a paint box and a stool. After their daughter, Ruth, was born, Martha turned to still lifes—milk pitchers, pears, everything tipping toward the background—until she dried up altogether. "I will paint the dome," he said pleasantly. He dipped his brush in water again and watched the dissipating gold.

She shrugged and dismissed him. "Don't forget—the books," she warned, then struggled with her box to the stairs. The building the Sargents had lived in all their married life was full of stairs; stairs from the bedrooms to the kitchen, more stairs from the kitchen to the street. Everyone now knew stairs were bad: you couldn't live in town with stairs when you got old.

He dabbed at his paint tin and set upon the white cupola on the lid of the dome, the toothpick bars of the widow's walk. Immediately he lost the uncomfortable sense of being an old man in his body and became all eye and hand, his hand painting and his eye watching the hand, learning from it. The spring in the bristle taught him where he was.

Morning brought Mr. Sargent again to the breakfast table. His lips moved as he sought the tone for a letter to his troubled daughter in Los Angeles. Why was Ruth so troubled and what troubled her? He didn't know. But it was serious enough that she left two daughters and a husband in Cambridge and fled to the far edge of the nation with a woman named Penelope. He had never said a disapproving word to Ruth; there were secret depths to the human heart, and he respected those. Asking anything of her was a delicate matter, but his friends were too old to be reliable, and Ruth was —she was his. He appealed to her as simply as he knew how, tried to be as clear as possible regarding his need. "Dear Deserter of the Effete East," he wrote, "esteemed *executrix*! I wonder if you will take an interest in the distribution of several hundred modest paintings? Your mother finds me 'compulsive' on this front—and she is keen to unload." Martha was downstairs again, in cahoots with the man from Skinner who was going to auction off the old silver because Ruth had written that, if it was all the same to the Sargents, she would rather have the money than the goods.

Mr. Sargent folded his letter, stamped it and laid it in the box, Outbound. This done, he resumed the pleasurable work of arranging his estate of watercolors. He found it best to view pictures hanging, so he began with the walls of his own bedroom, and moved down the narrow stairs that divided the sleeping from the living quarters, driving nails. He arranged his works up and down and across the walls of the room Ruth called—in jest—the Living Tomb, because of the heavy curtains Martha kept drawn to defend her mother's mahogany.

He walked up and down the thirteen stairs with care, fired inside by the thrill of living boldly. Paintings surrounded him in every room—excepting Ruth's old room, which Martha had occupied since Ruth moved out thirty years ago —his watercolors of the State House, the brownstone face of the Athenaeum, jetties and barns and bays in Maine, and worldly views from the Sargents' travels to ancient ports after Ruth had grown up and gone.

Martha's key rattled furiously in the lock. He rattled nails in his hand until her voice came up behind him. “My God, look what you’ve done. You’ve hammered new holes in the walls.” She put her hands on her hips and looked at him. Through the indefensible gold helmet of her thinning hair he saw pilgrims march across the wallpaper.

She served his dinner on a cheap cracked plate.

“Can’t we keep the Syracuse?” he asked.

“As a matter of fact, I sold off the whole lot to the china man,” she told him. “No more cooking! Frog Pond Village serves two meals a day.” He bent his head, acknowledging the paring down that brought one at last to the core. Frog Pond Village was a city of ancients. Nearly everyone they knew who was still alive lived there in apparently merry fellowship. They dined together in the vast dining room, took buses into Symphony. The daily death toll was posted on a cork board in the mail room. Martha couldn’t wait to get in.

For dessert she’d made his favorite whipped berry air pudding, which he took as a sign of the strength of her old affections, as a sign that she had, for now, kept the eggbeater.

She blew fog at him across the top of her Styrofoam cup of tea. “I had better sponge and press your dark suit,” she said. “Kay Kilcannon’s funeral is Tuesday at two.” Kay Kilcannon, mowed down by a van on Huntington Avenue coming out of Symphony Hall, was as good as a brochure for Frog Pond Village. But Martha, having scored her point already, said no more.

Besides a few sticks of furniture Martha wanted everything out of the little room he called his “office.” If he wanted to save any of the papers in his old file cabinet, then he ought to send them to Ruth.

Mr. Sargent’s papers consisted of letters he had typed over

the years on his Model 5, and letters from several eminent poets and painters to whom he had written in friendship or hope. On top of these effects he laid Volumes One and Two of his journals and sketches from the war (he'd driven an ambulance in Italy), and a copy of his mimeographed and stapled *Selected Verse.* Inside the front sheet he wrote:

> To Ruth: I convey these scraps of life (and me)
> to keep as you will, or give to posterity.

He walked two blocks to the post office in the belly of the State House and handed the packet to the postmistress. In the broad pink circle of her face Mr. Sargent saw the classical composition of a round family portrait: the father, himself, and the mother, surrounding the child in the protective bubble of the whole.

How much did he want of immortality, anyway? *The play of Sargent's wit on the underbelly of the world casts the kind of shadows lightning makes*—that would be kindness to hear. But truthfully, Mr. Sargent understood that any possible interest in his selected verse would be posthumous, and he agreed that it should. Death was needed to justify the broad claims a poet made for life. A red ribbon ran through his hands, and through Ruth's hands, and beyond her also, into her children's hands, and fluttered out behind them all, running on, a ribbon, continuous. The red ribbon fluttered out behind them all.

Some men have visions of the Angel of Death, or stand on bridges and see their bodies fallen and smashed on the water below. Mr. Sargent's vision of Death was colored by family lore, which on this subject was particularly vivid. He saw his Uncle Art, still fairly sound in his mind, lying on his back longways on the ties of the old Boston & Maine line inland from the family's summer place on Black Island Harbor, his eyes closed and his head raised above the dust on a pair of black dress shoes. That train no longer ran, the old Bostons having died off and the young ones, who had no interest in beating old horsehair mattresses each June, having deserted. All his life Mr. Sargent had envisioned Death coming this way: a train arriving and an old man waiting.

Now, however, in the round face of the postmistress, Mr. Sargent saw a new end. His daughter would come, the prodigal would return; he saw two reddish figures speaking simply in a darkened room. Lying quiet between white sheets, Mr. Sargent would speak to Ruth; simple words would come to him that would redeem them both from whatever had gone so wrong. Ruth would confide in him, he would nod and understand—he felt he understood already, whatever the broad outlines of her struggle—and she would be surprised and grateful, and he would close his eyes.

Then his verse would speak.

"First class or book rate?" the postmistress called over her meter. In the rumbling hams of her cheeks he saw the movement of all flesh.

Ruth's reply arrived the following week in a manila envelope addressed to him in blocky handwriting. Her letter read, in part: "Thanks for trusting me. Regarding the paintings, I am [a word here seemed to be missing] by your trust! But you're not dead yet! Can't you get some storage at Frog Pond Village?" Also in the envelope Mr. Sargent found two volumes of *New Lesbian Detective Stories* with bright-colored covers, and a scrawl on a bookmark: "Welcome to the new world, Dad. (Ha, ha.)"

While he'd waited for his daughter to tell him the fate of

his paintings, Martha won the argument over literature. "Prune! Prune!" she cried daily, and obediently Mr. Sargent lined brown boxes with Dr. Johnson, Keats and the brothers James. He filled other boxes with Hawthorne and Hardy and noble Homer. He had begun at the beginning, with Aeschylus and Auden and continued on through Bacon and Balzac, Coleridge (That sunny dome! Those caves of ice!), Conrad, Cozzens and both Cranes, then on to Dickens and Dos Passos, Emerson, Empson, Fitzgerald, Flaubert and Fielding. With a few exceptions, he found that "pruning" did not overly concern him. He looked at the debauched shelves and at the books piled on the floor.

The two volumes Ruth had sent lay in a box. On a whim he plucked one up and tried to read it. He sat down at the breakfast table, where the best light was for reading, but something put him off—the brightness, the womanishness, the genre, the subject and the style. It seemed to be all women talking tough; he found no center to it. He imagined Ruth in her old room, reading this, eating something crumbly in bed, her door wide open for anyone to see—*New Lesbian Detective Stories*—chuckling merrily to herself. She was always, in his recollection of her, eating something crumbly, or else she was running it off, or just coming in from a run, standing in the kitchen eating a muffin, damp-looking in shorts and a torn T-shirt, her legs an alarming shade of red. Martha always advised moderation and no food between meals, but Ruth was not like Martha. "I have to work like an ox," Ruth told him once when he asked her what was the point of running nowhere. As usual when Ruth explained her reasons, he could only stare at her. Where had she come from? *I have to work like an ox.* Yet she ate muffins in bed and read the morning away—did she still? Her leaving the girls and Len the way she did was too painful to talk about (there were secret depths to the human heart, and he would not question those). The girls were grown up now in any case, and they had turned out very *satisfactory,* as Martha said. Ruth was simply a larger-than-life figure, exuberant, unnatural, and he felt that he understood her, she was like him, an intensified version of himself—oxlike.

The word *thighs* leered up at him from the bottom of a page. He stopped reading and put Ruth's book to one side, satisfied that he had dipped in, that he had communicated with Ruth in a better way than he could by letter or, God forbid, on the telephone. He picked up *Moby Dick* and skimmed the opening chapters—met again the cannibal Queequeg, reread the black tablets in the chapel in New Bedford, which told the fate of the whalemen. Mr. Sargent lost himself for a time in Dickens—who wrote less well than Thackeray, but had (someone said this) *more news.* Mr. Sargent laughed out loud in his chair at the life of Chuzzlewit and the hypocrite Pecksniff, and read the morning away.

Martha came in empty-handed and discovered him there. She stopped abruptly on the threshold when she saw him, her brown eyes wide. She had more of the beauty of Art than of Nature, but she used a subtle pot of face paints, and her gold helmet of hair was a touching, persistent little lie. "Good afternoon," he said.

"I can't feed you," she said.

He smiled. "You'd leave me to starve?"

"There's nothing for lunch," she said loudly. She stood frozen in the doorway. He might have been a ghost.

"No trouble—I'll feed at the sandwich shop!" he said.

He walked downstairs and around the corner. The cold stabbed him and the brightness of the street made him feel vague and undefined by contrast. His legs seemed soft. But when he went inside the sandwich shop and sat down on the familiar red banquette his appetite returned and he ordered a cup of fish chowder, a small salad and a muffin. The muffin was tasty and the soup delicious—the commonplace lifted to the sublime—thickened with flour, not cream, and salted with the familiar complex of powders he had come to appreciate from Campbell's cans. His salad lay in pale concavities of iceberg lettuce, which he preferred to other kinds because it gave less of the bovine sense of grass between his teeth.

After lunch he ordered a dish of ice cream. The bones thrummed in his skull, an amplifying ache. Was he ill at all? There was a touch of incontinence, but he would not complain. He wanted to live in the same way he wanted to remain at table, not because he was starving, or craved a sweet at the end, but because he took pleasure in living. He had held a few things up in his hands in his time, so that people could see them. What had he held up, what had he shown? Least bitterns and grebes among the cattails in Olmstead's Fens, a Hepplewhite chair seen through a shallow bow window and a lavender pane, the old delivery truck from Pierce's, the Christmas Eve candles in the window on Mount Vernon and West Cedar Streets, the commanding presence of the gold dome, sloops in Black Island Harbor and the little mailboat with a bone in her teeth! He had shown what he had seen, his place in his time. Why this rush to clear the mess from your own last supper?

Pulling himself up from the banquette he knocked the ice cream dish to the floor. It crashed and rattled upside down, intact. Bending to pick it up he read the manufacturer's stamp on the back: Syracuse. It made his hair stand on end.

He tried all afternoon to lose himself in Dickens, in the

jolly gin-swilling deathbed nurse, Mrs. Gamp, but the ache in his head compelled him to lie down with his eyes closed and look at a hot ball of white in the darkness. The pain was so intense that no idea or image could punctuate it. Toward evening Martha came into his room and closed the door firmly behind her. He opened his eyes and was horrified by the vividness of her color, by the pineapple post at the foot of his bed and the saber legs of his side chair, and by the blade of her outstretched hand with two pills on it. *Nurse Gamp!* His mouth hung open; he had forgotten how to close it.

"Tablets for your headache," she called to him in the ringing, overloud tone of a street-corner salvationist begging alms for the poor.

"Come on!" she urged him, rattling the pills. "It's nothing heroic."

The next morning he rose for Kay Kilcannon's funeral and shaved in the bath, savoring the heft of his mortar of foam and his bristle brush. When he returned to his room to dress she had made his bed and laid out his clothes, exactly as he would wear them: dark suit around a shirt, the red ribbon of his bow tie, and hanging down the side of the bed, his trousers. On the floor his shoes and inside each shoe, a sock. The only thing missing was himself. He looked between the points of the collar, at the empty hole where his head would be, at the dun-colored humps of the bedspread.

He dressed, then went to look for her. He needed her to tie the silk bow around his neck, but she had closed herself in the bath to "make up." He was about to step out of her bedroom, which he still thought of as Ruth's, but instead he stopped and looked around him. Quietly, secretly, he pulled the flapping brass rings on the dresser drawers. The drawers held little—a comb, a rope of pearls, a bed jacket in a plastic wrapper with the sleeves folded across the front, a smell of violets. In the top drawer he found, stunningly, his old pipe and a drawing. Martha had not done anything in years, but he recognized the subject, an odd little man who used to rent bungalows near the Sargents' old summer place in Maine. The story about the man was that years ago he shot and nearly killed his wife. She remained true to him, however. This figure was definitely he, sitting on a wood block in front of a shack whose roof was an upturned dory. He wore a woolen shirt and dirty trousers and seemed to be looking at the artist—at Martha—with dull, violent eyes, one larger than the other. Where had Martha gotten this—vision? It was most certainly hers; behind the man and the shack a hill rolled dangerously backward, and the large birch trees at the top of the painting angled strangely and threatened the tiny trees she had drawn in at the bottom. She certainly couldn't have gotten it sitting on a stool. Mr. Sargent brought the drawing close to his eyes and then held it at arm's length. The thing was the expression of the man, together with the vertiginous vanishing point, the whole in a rather cunning disequilibrium. How had she seen it? How had she known? But the man—his name was Burns, an old local name—didn't live under a dory. He lived at some bungalows with his wife. The drawing was very good around the eyes particularly, and overall there was something—cunning in it. But he dismissed it finally as romantic; the bucket of potatoes at the man's feet was a heavy touch. Mr. Sargent laid the drawing back in the drawer, but on an impulse removed the pipe and put it in his pocket. He pushed the bow front closed; the brass rings ticked against the wood. A flash of red caught the corner of his eye and he turned around, guilty, but it was only a cardigan in her closet, hanging from a bar.

In church he forgot who had died. The old Wurlitzer spun out a dirge, and his head filled with darkness. Where was his wife? He looked wildly around him, but could not find her among the formidable women who stood erect in the middle pews. There she was, of course, right beside him: his wife, who never used a puff, who powdered her face with two fingers; who would put a dose of sherry in tomato soup; who had a certain rigid gusto for living. He reached over suddenly and covered her hand with his, part tenderness, part ballast. Her fingers on the spine of the hymnal had the contours of twigs.

"Blessed is the man whose strength is in thee," Father Black read from the Psalms. "Who passing through the valley of Baca make it a well; the rain also filleth the pools." Then they sang. Her vibrato trembled high above the hymn; through the cracks in her golden helmet he saw her jeweled ear, her skull; he saw her eyes cup tears.

Home from church, she pulled his class book from a box. "This book has your picture in it," she said. "Do you want it for anything or shall I chuck it?" He took the class book from her, the only book to which he had ever confided the scope of his ambitions, and weighed it in his hand. A sticky moss of dust hugged the buckram, but the heft of the book reminded Mr. Sargent, oddly, of himself, and how easy it would be to pin the donkey tail on that ox of a man! He studied his wife's face for irony, but she was subtly painted as ever, and perfectly composed. In truth, he could think of no real use for the book, if it came to that. He handed it back to her, unopened.

"Chuck it," he agreed.

Undressing, he found the old pipe still in his pocket. Why had he taken it? Where could he hide it? He opened his drawers, but she rooted through them regularly, adding and subtracting undershirts and socks. Under his mattress? Such extreme stealth was distasteful to him, and besides, it was not inconceivable that, stick as she was, she might turn the mattress over sometime. (She insisted that the pillow of a grown man be aired on the back windowsill two hours a day.) At the old summer place in Maine she used to heave whole blue-ticked mattresses over the fenceposts and beat them with the handle of a broom. But the place was boarded up now, held in trust for the far-flung children on his brother's side.

He turned the pipe over in his hands. It still stank, pleasantly, of his blend. Mr. Sargent had never seen himself as a ruddy man on a dock, but the pipe erased any doubt: there it was, clamped in his teeth. He was one of several ruddy men in corduroy trousers on a dock, smoking their pipes, surrounded by thermoses of sherried soup and ladies' straw hats, everything old from many summers. Martha was there too, as were the Van Thiels and the Blodgetts. They happened to be standing on the dock the day the young Burns boy and his girl tried to tie up their little day sailer and come ashore. It was out of the question, of course. "What do you want here?" Mr. Sargent had called out, courteous, of course, but proprietary. "We just want to walk around," said the boy.

"We can't have you ashore," Mr. Sargent told him. "The island is privately owned." The look in the boy's eye as he yanked the sheet at the last moment—that was the look, wasn't it, that Martha got in her drawing? Fury—real feeling! He himself had never rendered it. The little boat grew small on the harbor, the little triangle of jib pointed at the dairy bar on the big island. He had imagined the boy telling his father—the man who shot his wife—"We tried to tie up at Private Island but the Bostons told us to go away." He had thought even then it wouldn't hurt to let the boy and his girl come ashore. But of course he couldn't allow it.

Mr. Sargent had no use now for a pipe. He tossed it into one of the boxes Martha had prepared for the Ladies' Aid.

"Who will take all these pictures?" Her vibrato rose an octave, reaching Mr. Sargent in the kitchen.

"Why don't you take the State House, Helen? You could hang it on that bare spot in your hall." Mr. Sargent heard his wife's voice while he stood at the kitchen counter and poured a prepared martini and a scotch over ice from the tiny bottles people bought on planes.

The Collinses sat in the living room, which was deep-sounding now that Martha had emptied the shelves and sold off the rug. She no longer saw any real reason to entertain, but the Collinses were great friends of poor Kay Kilcannon, who, before she was struck and crushed by a van, often had Ted and Helen in for Sunday supper. Before the Collinses arrived Mr. Sargent had arranged the tiny bottles the way he used to arrange the fifths in the kitchen—three martinis, three scotches and two demis of Rhine wine. He used to line up the fifths on the silver-plated tray with the cocktail shaker and the ice bucket and the ice tongs and the jigger.

Those fifths of liquor on the silver-plated tray with the cocktail shaker and the gleaming tools had formed one of the important pleasures of his life. It was a pleasure on a par with greeting Queequeg to make perfect cocktails with the proper tools and the correct ingredients, to complete a work, and to present it this way, publicly.

On a well-used cocktail napkin he scribbled with his pen:

Absent friends, cocktail time;
Flood of memory, river of rhyme

and covered it up with his drink. He carried the cocktails on a battered red tin tray and handed them down to the Collinses and Martha.

"We went to three funerals this week alone," Helen said, rolling the *r* in her *three* slightly. "Barbara Beery called me up on Saturday morning and asked me to walk with her, on account of her eyes. She said everyone on Mount Vernon Street is dead."

"Is that true?" cried Martha.

Helen counted on her ringed fingers: "The Bob Thorntons, both, Ellen Cuddehey, Kipper Raven, Cogswell, and now Kay Cloud."

"It's Kay Kil*cannon,*" Martha said quickly.

"Oh, good night! Kilcannon, I mean."

"And Dave Van Thiel," Ted put in.

"Ted and Helen are going to take the State House," Martha told Mr. Sargent when he handed down her glass of wine.

He held the empty tray flat against his heart to signal he was rent. "The gilded dome!" he said, but with great feeling, so they would know he didn't mean it. The four of them looked at the picture hanging on the wall between views of sunset on the mall and a starboard-tacking day sailer on Black Island Harbor.

"Let's take it down now and put it by the door," Martha said.

"That would be just great," said Helen.

Ted leapt to his feet. He was always eager to perform some human task, eulogies, pallbearing.

*

November brought gray weather and wind. She pulled down his paintings and gave them away, or packed them, mysteriously, for "storage." She left the nails in the walls. Mr. Sargent tried to be helpful; he stayed out of her way and read a great deal from books he remembered having enjoyed before. Much as he enjoyed rereading these books, he could not, the moment he finished them, recall which books they were. Martha tried to send him out to do this or that, but he said he found the weather cool since the Ladies' Aid snagged his London Fog. The truth was he could no longer get a fair footing on the frost-heaved bricks, and even the stairs caused trouble.

Patience be a tired mare, thought Mr. Sargent (Shakespeare said it), yet she will plod. Martha bought frozen dinners two at a time and, lacking a book or knitting, twined her fingers in her lap and stared out the windows at the familiar view. What she was waiting for—the peculiar force behind her patience—came to Mr. Sargent slowly, like the deep layer of a good book after years of rereading.

One evening in early December he supped lightly on cold cereal and milk, then climbed the stairs. Martha was combing her hair in her dresser mirror; he waved goodnight to her reflection through the door. He dressed carefully in underwear and pajamas. Then he climbed into the bed and pulled the white sheets up to his chin. Through the window he saw the dome as he had seen it every night, illuminated in the darkness, hovering outside his window like a spaceship, blotting out the river and the sky. He began to recite to himself—it was his way of counting sheep:

> It was a robber's daughter, and her name was Alice Brown,
> Her father was the terror of a small Italian town . . .

He broke off, distracted, and looked for a pattern of nails in the walls. Finding none, he closed his eyes and lifted his fingers humbly to his face, blind, using the spring-touch sense of his fingers to see. He painted over his face with the ends of his fingers and tried to see the ruddy man he hadn't seen for years.

Heels tapped the floor like a fingernail on a windowpane, then Martha stepped into his room and stood beside his bed in her red cardigan and a skirt. Mr. Sargent looked up and barely knew her. He took his hands from his face and raised them above his chest in a prayerful attitude to keep, he felt, the paint off the sheets. She sat down on the straight-backed chair beside his bed and put a handful of bent fingers on his shoulder. She leaned close to his ear. "You haven't been an easy man, Bill," she said, "but I've been faithful to you. You probably never questioned it." She took his hands in hers and gripped them tightly. He closed his eyes, and when he opened them again, she had left him.

"Faithful?" he said. But no one answered. He clenched his teeth as if to clasp his pipe against a sudden jarring.

A round light punctured the dark and found him, sweeping him up in a wide, white circle. From far away, then closer, Mr. Sargent felt the shudder and heard the scream. But it was not what he expected. He climbed stiffly from his bed to investigate the noise and found his wife fallen on the narrow stairs, crumpled over a brittle bone in her hip, calling his name. Later he learned that hips are the weakness of old women; helping her back onto her feet and upstairs to bed was the worst thing he could have done.

Black Book

THE BUMPS ON HER ARMS infatuate Ruth. She scratches them with a bitten fingernail, raising the stakes. The bumps could be something she picked up from the gym: hives or nerves or the flesh-eating virus. They could be ringworm, or those parasites that live in the feathers of pigeons, eat through stucco and earthquake netting, then burrow in your body and ream you like a lemon. On the other hand, maybe her body's projecting something: Ruth's fifty today, and naturally her thoughts have turned to decay and death, and romantic prospects for the future. But she's lost her black book, her agenda, and what hope has a woman of fifty without names, phone numbers, and a plan?

She used to know red bumps—how many nights did she sit up late with Dr. Spock flattened on her knees, eating this or that from Len's mom's store and drinking stout, reading about rubeola on a child's trunk? But she has thrown that book away, or rather she left it in Cambridge with Len and the girls ten years ago when she threw that life away—*Baby and Child Care* stuck in the shelf behind the telephone table with the *Nutrition Almanac* and the Zagat guide, and the yellow pad engraved with urgent scribbles and the urn of dead pens.

She and Len used to sit up late in bed, eating cupcakes from the store and talking about problems: money, the children, Ruth's enfeebled parents on Beacon Hill, Ruth's girlfriend, and how soon Ruth could move with her to the West Coast. They—Ruth and Len—slept together in their crumbs. For some reason Ruth remembers that part rather fondly. Now her daughters, both functioning, independent-living attorneys, tell Ruth that Len has blown up like a whale. He puts away doughnuts and falafels as if they were M&Ms. Two years ago when Ruth went back East to visit she saw to her disappointment that it was true, Len *was* gaining weight: she even found a can of mixed nuts on the edge of the bathtub. Her parents weren't doing so well either. They seemed gaunt and stranger than usual, probably starving to death from politeness. But what could she do, besides read over the fine print on their quarterly statements, cook a chicken, impress upon them the danger of stairs and the wisdom of annual tax-free gifts to herself and the girls? She hasn't been back since.

The girls come to California for a couple of rushed visits a year, usually traveling on business. They turned out well—concert-going, self-supporting—and overall Ruth is glad she bolted and broke away, or else she would certainly have thrown herself into the river, and what would the girls have done with that? But this life in Los Angeles, in Venice, actually—where a woman can lift weights on the beach and pump bullets into the outline of a man—is not so new anymore. It's full of insipid disagreements, like any life. Recently, on a quick gambling trip to Reno, Ruth discovered her ex-girlfriend Vick using her toothbrush, rubbing it all over her teeth and her tongue and the roof of her mouth because, she claimed, she had forgotten her own. Vick actually had a vile fungus, which she passed on to Ruth, who had to take a ten-day course of antibiotics. Maybe that's where the bumps came from.

There's always the fear, Ruth thinks now, that one thing leads to another, fate might be linked to conduct: that's what guilt is about. But Ruth is not, *au fond*, guilty—just self-involved—she knows that much about herself. She runs her fingers over the bumps once more, then washes her hands at the kitchen sink with Joy, fastens on her fanny pack and heads out to the market to pick up extra food for her party later on. The party is women only, but without her black book Ruth could only invite the traceable ones, the ones she could track down easily, through the usual channels, the gym and the phone book, and where's the sport in that? It's her birthday, and if she's not free now to change her mind or lower the bar, then when? Some of the women coming are, like Ruth herself, of the meridian, the dangerous years; there are a couple of really young ones too.

At the market Ruth sees an acquaintance named Gerd Tinglum. Gerd works at Ruth's gym as a personal trainer, but Ruth would never go that far one-on-one—too fat! Gerd must be fifty-five at least, but she looks boyish and clean from her days of prophylactic labor; her arms look like carved stone. Ruth eats purple figs from a brown paper sack and rolls her cart from side to side down the aisles, flirting and impinging upon Gerd, pursuing her. Gerd does not withdraw, and Ruth invites her to the party, shrewdly not mentioning which birthday.

"Let me guess what you like," Ruth interrupts herself. "Ryvita, right? Goat cheese? Dried fruit?"

Gerd the Fit, as Ruth thinks of her, looks Ruth in the eye with thrilling directness, sucks in her breath and sings "*Ja-a.*" Ruth rolls her cart from side to side, exuding, she hopes, an aura of health and vigor. Furtively she plucks up a bottle of homeopathic pills for the bumps on her arm. She is going to pop them in her pocket and protest the system that way, but she remembers that honesty is sometimes a virtue with women, and how humiliating it was the time she got caught with a package of batteries. Gerd instantly picks up the bottle of pills from the belly of the cart and reads the label, then cocks her head at Ruth and says, "You have a rash? I vill have a look!" Ruth raises her eyes to meet Gerd's arctic gaze, and smiles. This is certainly fair warning to Gerd, in case Ruth is contagious.

Ruth kneels on her futon and rewinds her answering machine until the red light glows. Having her bumps read by Gerd turned out to be less awful than Ruth feared. Gerd's professional judgment: adult acne brought on by the antibiotics Ruth took for a fungus—it will pass. Now Gerd sits at Ruth's white tin table, captured in an amber light. She's fifty-five at minimum, but tightly built; her silver hair is spiky and she's machine-tanned. Lemon Zinger in a cup steams up around her as she leans forward, forced to hear the complicated stories that wind out of Ruth's machine.

Lu calls. She and Vick are both coming to the party—they wouldn't miss it. The next message is from Vick, who obviously isn't communicating very well with Lu. Vick says they definitely are *not* coming—she has to stay home by the phone drinking cancer tea and waiting for word that her lump is benign.

Leslie's message says, "The dog's dead—I'll be there." Last year Leslie missed Ruth's birthday party because Ruth wouldn't let her bring her dog, and the year before that, well, Ruth doesn't really remember.

Ruth stands up on her futon now, her feet in socks, and makes notes next to names on a yellow legal pad; it's all she has to go by. Next to Vick's name she writes *cancer?* and next to Leslie's *dog dead.* Her inner arm itches with adult acne induced by—Vick? She scratches it on her jeans.

The last message is from her mother in Boston. "Ruth! Is this the answering service? This is Ruth's mother calling. Please tell Ruth her mother and her father called from Boston to wish her a happy birthday. Would you ask her to call, please, and *reverse the charges*—" The rest of the message is blotted out by Gerd's Norse voice: "I have not so many vimen in my life! You got them all in your bed?"

Ruth snickers and waves the women off the ends of her fingers. The telephone rings again and Ruth lets the machine pick up the call. It's Penelope from San Francisco. Penelope says, "Ruth? Ruth, it's Penelope calling from San Francisco! Are you there, Ruth . . . ? I'll wait until your machine cuts me off in case you're in the—" Ruth lifts the receiver and leans over her desk, scribbling on her yellow pad and speaking into the receiver in a low voice. Then she hangs up abruptly and comes back to the table, joining Gerd.

"Penelope, Penelope, I might know her," Gerd says. "Skinny one, young? Lifts weights?"

Ruth lifts a sliver of mango from a plate. It's slick as a goldfish in her fingers. "You might," she admits. "I haven't seen her for a year. She's manic, usually, but the lid came off in a big way. I mean, she ended up spying on me with this tiny red telescope, if you know what I'm saying." Ruth squints through an imaginary telescope to show the dimensions. "Finally I had to call the police. There were no limits, you know what I mean? She lives in San Francisco now, but she might be coming back."

"*Ja, ja.*" Gerd nods vigorously and sucks in her breath.

"Maybe I was wrong," says Ruth. "I mean, everybody's got a psychology, right? I could have gone outside the system, hired someone—"

Gerd isn't following. "I know Penelope. She vas going to give me a little dope to teach her how to go on the roller blades."

"Roller blades! Ha!" Ruth laughs, imagining Penelope, her shocked-looking moon face rolling toward Gerd Tinglum on Ocean Front Walk, her arms straight out in front, her kneecaps bleeding. But Ruth has never taken Penelope lightly, and now—time to change the subject! It's almost one o'clock. She switches on a CD of clanging Berlioz, the *Symphonie Fantastique,* and ascends the little step to her kitchen. Her fingers range across the counter; she pulls a lemon from a paper bag and tosses the bag out behind her.

Ruth pounds out some garlic with the dull side of a blade and peels it in her fingers. Her hands run energetically over the turkey to spread the garlic and to open up the rosemary needles she pulled earlier from some landscaping at the architect's next door. She sprays salt and coarse pepper with a generous hand, whips up an egg and pours it into a nest of seasoned breadcrumbs, spoons stuffing into the cavity. Then she goes to the sink and scrubs her hands with hot soapy water; you can't be too careful after touching a bird.

*

Ruth moves around her tiny kitchen, closing the refrigerator door with her hip, scratching her itchy arms on her shorts, polishing drinking glasses on her black T-shirt, opening tins, opening cheese, scratching. Gerd interrupts with advice about breathing with the body. She shows Ruth how to loosen the muscles in her neck and roll her head around her shoulders, and how to pull her abdomen toward her backbone with her breath. Ruth is interested, to a point. She even gets down on the floor next to Gerd and tries to raise a leg over her stomach and touch the floor on the far side. But she just feels stuck, like a bug on its back.

"You are so tight!" Gerd chides her. "Not like me, feel!" She places Ruth's hand on the veined ball of her shoulder, then leaps into a squatting position, peeling off a layer of spandex. "Let's get loose!" But Ruth has to get the potatoes on; a clock inside her is ticking. Besides, she remembers the extra skin around her middle, and decides that night would definitely be a better time to get down to anything on the floor with Gerd.

Gerd amuses herself for a time, playing with the toys and trinkets Ruth keeps around, and Ruth, preoccupied with vegetables, actually loses track of Gerd in the room. She's surprised to look up and see Gerd at the door. "Ruth, I am going," Gerd shouts over the music. She pronounces it "Root."

Ruth worries suddenly that she hasn't tried hard enough —that she hasn't really tried at all. She jumps off the kitchen step and heads toward her guest, clutching a carrot and a green peeling device in her hands. "Why don't you stay for the party? Or you could come back later?"

"*Ja, ja,* maybe I vill," says Gerd.

"Wait," pleads Ruth, walking right past Gerd toward her bed and her desk, around which she keeps all her records in incoherent piles. "I need to write down your number." She holds the carrot and the green peeler in one hand and with the other sends birthday greetings, matchbooks and coins to the floor. "Hold on! Hold on!"

"Hey, don't worry about it. I see you later."

Ruth instantly identifies a certain note in Gerd's voice as insincerity. A flume of music suddenly crashes down the walls behind her. "Shouldn't we get together again? I mean, should we?" Ruth calls across the room.

Gerd lingers over three silver dollars in a bowl near the door. "*Ja,* Root. Call me." She turns the coins over and over in her fingers; they reappear and disappear.

"Well, you could, if you *would.*" Ruth looks down at her knees, which are inexplicably scabbed and red. She looks up to see Gerd pull a pencil from her jacket pocket and scribble a telephone number on the wall.

The potatoes roll around in their boiling water. It's nearly a relief, not to find herself *déshabillé* on the floor with Gerd. Ruth thinks again of Penelope, how young she still is, round in the face and tractable in certain ways. Ruth envisions her powder-blue Volkswagen bus vibrating at the curb outside some rented pastel box in the flatlands while Penelope throws her stuff in back—beef jerky, marijuana, trail mix and water for a week. It's easy to romanticize Penelope now, but even the best times were usually disappointing—curling up on Zuma Beach at sunset under Penelope's multicolored orlon afghan, which turned out to be alive with lice. One time they drove down the coast together, Penelope at the wheel because Ruth had a terrible sty in her eye.

Voices made her head itch, Penelope said. "What do they say?" Ruth asked. She appreciated a lurid imagination, that fine line between reckless invention and total schizophrenia.

Penelope immediately closed her eyes and said in a flat tenor voice, "The naked throng at Albion eschewed the hogshead until, still drumming at dawn, they bore into the face with their pacifist chopsticks and carved out the several meanings of hunger. The boy in the garden crept among the farm-animals with the gun in his hand that tamed the West."

That was interesting: the Penelope Ruth knew would never say "naked throng" or "eschewed" or "crept among." Ruth always suspected that Penelope's medieval take on things came from some experience or drug, or some real place up north, which Ruth herself might like to explore sometime.

The ride was thrilling. One side of the road was ragged rock over the ocean—a moment of road followed by a moment of air. Five hundred feet below, the deep ocean foamed. Above, mountains the color of lions, dun-colored, rose at an obtuse angle. Ruth said, *If snow be white, why then your breasts are dun,* and Penelope laughed. Tears ran down her cheeks, she laughed so hard. The side of Ruth's face throbbed, a kind of heightened consciousness, however miserable. Penelope laughed and Ruth laughed along, removing with the end of one finger a string of white goop that had gathered in the corner of her infected eye.

Penelope suddenly stopped the car in the middle of nowhere and scrubbed furiously at her scalp with both hands. "They're calling me," she said. "It's too loud." She covered her head with her afghan and wouldn't come out until Malibu. Ruth was unwilling to drive along these dangerous cow-covered cliffs one-eyed, with no perception of depth. But in the end she had to, because Penelope couldn't get a grip.

*

At a few minutes before three o'clock Ruth stands in the shower under a pulse of water and sings everything that comes into her lungs—a piece from *Figaro:*

All call for me
All want me
"I need a wig"
"I want a shave,"

a one-part version of "Frère Jacques." She's careful to keep her green apple soap away from her arms, which sting under water. The red bumps stand up in peaks now, each distinct and hooded with a tiny scab. She thinks of Karl Marx and his painful carbuncles getting in the way of his work on *Das Kapital*—or inspiring it, maybe—and how he took arsenic to keep them down. Ruth married Len while she was still infatuated with Marx—or, to be truthful, while she was infatuated with a young lesbian at college who was infatuated with Marx. What Ruth loved best about politics was the almost feminine beauty of the young socialists, the rebellious curl of their ardent, swollen lips quoting Marx, Debs. She enjoyed the rallies, the rage, the furious longing. Marx, it turned out, was only obliquely Jewish; in fact he was anti-Semitic. And Len, who was emphatically and even a little religiously Jewish, didn't really want to hand over the means of production to the workers; he wanted to franchise out his mom's store. Ruth married him anyway, at nineteen, as a sort of compromise—defecting with a Jewish capitalist instead of a dyke—and shocked her parents, who of course forgave her. Ruth still has her old copy of *Kapital* around here somewhere; though she never got past the first few riveting chapters, she underlined almost every line she did read with red pen, permanently marking out her sympathies with ideas she remembers only dimly. On the other hand, now that her parents are too old to pull their own 1099s, Ruth has become more interested in economics. She has capital gains to look out for, and keeps an eye on the fortunes of Lorillard, Kraft, and Sarah Lee.

Ruth steps out of the tub and goes directly to her desk where, still dripping, she scribbles a note: *Call Mom.* She dries naturally, without a towel, while catching a few minutes of the financial news on TV. Then she dresses for her party in a white T-shirt, an orange silk shirt that covers most of the bumps, blue jeans, running shoes.

Ruth keeps the front door open to let in the wind and fresh air. Leslie, Lu and Vick arrive at three on the dot with a huge lemon cake and sing "Happy Birthday" to Ruth in the doorway. The word CANCER hangs above Vick's head in black block letters, followed by a question mark. Ruth blinks, disbelieving, but Vick just sighs. "You won't believe this—now my biopsy is missing. A nurse called this morning and told me not to wait around. So here I am."

"Well, that's good, right?" Ruth's all compassion. Who wouldn't be?

"Leslie's been so helpful," says Vick. "She says I'm lucky I didn't want a kid, like she did. Isn't that sensitive?"

"Did you want a kid?" asks Leslie.

Vick's eyes fill with tears. "If I definitely can't have one I sure do!"

"Come, come!" says Lu. "It's a party, right?"

Other women arrive, come in and go out again, climb the steps to the roof to smoke their little clay pipes among the jade plants and look down at the bodybuilders on the beach. Two women, both quite young, quite good-looking—probably friends of Leslie's from the Jewish Sisterhood—come in with a birthday present: a red clay plate covered with black grapes. The woman holding the plate has jet black, Egyptian-looking hair and Indonesian clothes; her friend looks like a man. The Egyptian woman helps herself to some of the grapes and chews them with small, even teeth, reading the room casually. Ruth walks toward them to introduce herself. But then, suddenly shy, she draws back and just watches the women together, listening to their loud, intimate conversation, as if they were a play.

Egyptian Woman: I am going crazy with this hemorrhoid. It just hangs there—like a button.

The Man: A button?

Egyptian Woman: It probably isn't that big. It feels like a basketball hanging there when I walk. When I'm walking, I have to reach down and . . .

The Man: Tuck it back in?

Egyptian Woman: Tuck it in, exactly.

Ruth knows what they're talking about, all right—excruciating pain! The skull beneath the skin! She's about to make some remark when they wander inside and take the plate of grapes with them. Apparently they don't even realize that Ruth is the host.

These two remind Ruth of those parasites, *usufructuaries,* which ignore you as they use you, and don't hurt you in any way you'd notice. There are hundreds of examples from nature: barnacles on a whale's back; those lichens that inhabit the barest rocks, and live on rain and air. Ruth doesn't mind being used this way, being useful.

Ruth struggles with a bottle of zinfandel. Finally she uncorks it, pours some wine into a juice glass and gulps it down, wiping her mouth with her silk sleeve. She hardly ever gets drunk—why be fuddled when you could be acute?—but today she has a certain thirst in her mouth for these rich, bitter grapes from old vines. She splashes more wine into her glass and pours some for the others.

Penelope arrives at four, beautiful if just a little grimy, and humbly empty-handed. She throws her arms around Ruth, and says, "Happy birthday, Ruth," then pulls back, pressing Ruth's hands in her own cool, octopus hands, her fingers moving over Ruth's like suction cups. Penelope's scent—old clothes, fried chicken, pine trees—reminds Ruth with a sudden pungency why she will probably never have a really good relationship. Always there are problems, endless unanticipated sanitary or hygienic differences, or there are chemical dependencies with which Ruth has no patience at all, although she wouldn't mind scoring a little ounce of that excellent marijuana Penelope used to grow up north; maybe later she'll ask.

Penelope lets go of Ruth's hands and flings an arm around her shoulders. They stand in the doorway together and look at all the women stuffed into Ruth's little apartment. "Girls! Girls! Girls!" sings Penelope, her beautiful black eyes greedy and dangerously bright.

The women move around the food like dories at a dock, the hulls of their hips butting up against each other around the white tin table. They pick at the bird, the potatoes, the grapes with their fingers. Leslie, after a couple of glasses of wine, breaks down in tears and recounts in vivid detail the death of her dog, Harald—the heart like a basketball, the draining of the lungs. The dog died a month ago, and Leslie's still so depressed she's seeing her therapist three times a week. She feels guilty; when her mother died a year ago she wasn't nearly this broken up.

"How *is* whatshername—the shrink?" Ruth asks, trying to remember. She's got the name in her black book, and a phone number.

"Oh, Lydia—she's fine—sort of," says Leslie. "You know they've all got problems of their own. When Harald died I had a quiet little memorial dinner. So I invite my friends who loved Harald, and my shrink, of course. But it's like she's never used silverware! Her knife and fork just screeching on her plate—she's driving everybody crazy! Finally I say, 'Can't you just use your fingers, or chopsticks, Lydia?' I always use chopsticks—I don't like to put a fork in my mouth. But she kept hacking away, completely oblivious."

"And yet, without this person in your life, you're a suicide, right?" says Ruth, lifting the bottle up again and pouring wine around.

"I know. But I was furious. She kept mirroring it back to me, you know? I hate that. She said she didn't understand what I was asking her to do. Wouldn't you expect a professional, trained psychologist to know how to cut up a fish?"

"Not necessarily," says Ruth, pouring wine and remembering Vick, for example, who was so oblivious she could just pick up another person's toothbrush, invade a person that way, put another person's toothbrush in her own mouth—and just not get it.

Penelope pulls at some loose yarn at the bottom of her sweater and tells Ruth she might try to get her old job back at Disney. She misses the candy colors of L.A., the raw city and the blue Astroturf; she misses the fantasy, her old friends drawing together, channeling their sick private demons into cartoon characters everyone understands.

Ruth's heart jiggles in her chest. Fluff in a groove of Penelope's lip reminds Ruth of the seediness of Penelope's personal habits, her weird pungency and the oily heat her body gives off when she stays awake for days. Her face shines and she leans forward to give Ruth a tiny sucking kiss. When she pulls back the fluff in her lip is gone.

Her hands chatter maniacally at the ribbing of her sweater, yarn dribbles out behind her. "Ruth, I don't want to upset you, but tomorrow I'm going down to Disney and then I'm going to look at a room in Culver City."

"You're not moving in with Barb?" Ruth didn't even think to invite Barb to the party.

"I'm just looking. Barb said there's a room, completely separate. She's got an extra parking space for my bus in her garage."

"Did she say that?" Ruth thinks of all the junk she's had piled in Barb's garage since she moved into this single on the beach in June.

"Oh, you know, we've been talking about it," says Penelope vaguely. "I called her this morning."

"Did you tell her you were coming here?"

"I was oblique," says Penelope, her face shining like the time they first met.

Ruth's eyes fog over in shame. Somewhere she has the *I Ching* Barb gave her, with the five pennies inside. About a year ago, at Barb's insistence, Ruth moved hundreds of books and artifacts into Barb's garage, and Barb said, "No problemo, Ruth—I never use it," in a way that made Ruth feel she owed Barb something already. Then they played Scrabble until it was too late for Ruth to go home. Barb had a vase of blue delphiniums on the table beside the Scrabble board and they drank a special tea with lavender in it. Ruth remembers everything about that night, the words they crossed—*eccen-*

tric, captivating, bodywork, zendo, zydeco, orlon, Prozac, bamboozle, hara-kiri—and her own cowardly retreat after hours of assiduous groping. All her stuff is still there, unless Barb tired of looking at Ruth's treadmill and her electric foot massager and her boxes of detective novels and her waffle iron and threw it all out in a fit of pique.

"Yes, well. Look, maybe you should stay here tonight," Ruth hears herself say in the equivocal, deal-making voice she hates, but uses with Penelope. Ruth wouldn't put it past Penelope to try sleeping in her bus, even though anyone can see the neighborhood is worse than it used to be, and the bus is doubtless too pungent with dope not to attract junkies and fortune-seekers. As the host Ruth feels a certain responsibility for Penelope. And it's her birthday, after all.

Penelope smiles coyly and doesn't answer. She hands the pale blue end of a string of yarn to Ruth, then winks, and winds in and around the women, tied to Ruth that way, unraveling.

A tiny voice in Ruth's head says, "Maybe I vill see you later, Root." A reminder, that voice: what she really wants for her birthday is Gerd.

"Five minutes, Ruth, and then ready or not, we sing!" Lu calls out. The little kitchen is crammed with women working on the lemon cake. They shoo Ruth away and rummage in her drawers for a knife and forks. They cut up strawberries, whip some cream, arrange the cake on a plate and cover it with fifty-one candles. Happy Birthday, Happy Birthday, Happy Birthday.

Ruth retreats to her futon and sits with her back to her guests, weaving a cat's cradle from the blue yarn in her hand and looking at the ocean, the telephone at her ear like a shell.

It's not just women she can't reach; her black book has pages devoted to the migrations of her girls, their home and office phones and voice-mailboxes, their fax numbers and e-mail addresses and their boyfriends' names. The truth is, Ruth hasn't called them in months; she doesn't know how. The girls both sent cards, of course, and a couple of gifts Ruth hasn't opened yet, and probably they'll call on Sunday morning, one after the other. They are so organized.

Call Mom, Ruth thinks—it's much later in Boston than here. Ruth's mother sent a birthday check for $50—last year she sent $49. Ruth's father sent a "verse upon a birthday," which might be an allusion to some Greek poem, or it might be sincere and personal, who knows? Four minutes to cake: if she's going to call anyone, now's the time.

Gerd answers "*Ja*" on the first ring.

"It's me, Ruth," Ruth whispers into the telephone.

"*Ja,* I know," Gerd whispers back.

Ruth feels her heart beating inside her somewhere, ridiculously fervid.

"Root, I'm nothing but trouble. Vat do you vant with me?"

Outside her open window Ruth hears a siren. "What kind of trouble?" she asks.

"Who is it, Gerd?" A woman's shrill, accented voice comes near the telephone at the other end.

"Nobody, nothing, cut me some slack." Gerd's voice is no longer a whisper.

"They can't call here anymore," says the voice. "I've had it up to my neck!"

Ruth hears a physical struggle over the telephone receiver, which crashes against something hard. Then the unfamiliar voice is on the telephone, demanding, "Who is this speaking? I've had enough of this telephone business! What is your name?"

Ruth's caught short by the brutal, hollow, anonymous question. It goes in one ear and down those canals, freezing all the nerves in her face and pushing blood away from her heart in fast hydraulic whooshes that leave her thrumming, bloodless but wildly alive. "I'm Nobody—who are you?" Ruth says, recovering at once.

The Trouble with Money

THE MAIL BELONGED to Janie; it was her parallel universe and her literary life. Otherwise I would have gotten rid of the invitation to my son's wedding, torn it in half. Such is the unspeakable nature of a mother's love. But when I came back from the pharmacy with her diuretics and digoxin Janie already had everything spread out on the bed, catalogs, bills, magazines and the wedding invitation with its golden loopy writing on cardboard imprinted with a cheesy holographic rose. The card announced two o'clock nuptials in Birmingham, Alabama, and a reception to follow at the Velvet Turtle. The return envelope was already sealed and stamped on the nightstand, leaning up against the atomizer of Evian water Janie used to spray on her face.

She was incandescent from lack of circulation. "Willis is getting married in June," she said. "Now listen, Mum. We've got to go. It's important."

"Married at twenty-five?" I said. "How important could it be?"

"I want you to see him and meet his wife so when they have kids you'll know where they come from," she said.

I already knew where they'd come from. Birmingham! Janie must have been having heart surgery when they did history in school. Not that it mattered now. Willis was my son, but no one we knew. When he was seven I gave him to his father, a registered Republican who, after a few ordinary disappointments in Cambridge, fled "home" to Alabama. This was heartless and unnatural of me, I know, but the point is, I had to give my son up, for Janie. Now Willis was all the result of his upbringing, and I wasn't so interested anymore. My will was made up, no son mentioned.

"Let's send them an ice bucket and wish them a happy life," I told her.

"No, Mum. I talked to him. He really wants us. He wants you to come to his wedding."

"You spoke with Willis?" I couldn't see how. She'd never even met him.

"I called him up and asked if we were really invited. He's *nice,* Mum. He's my half brother. He even offered to pay."

That was somehow touching to hear—that my lost son would pay to see me. "What does he do for a living, he can afford to be such a dope?" I asked her.

"He's an aerobics teacher," she said, and climbed out of bed to let the fluid trapped in her chest run back down into her legs.

I laughed. Humor is important, and here in two words was everything I loved about injustice: it simplified life, and taught you who your enemies were. I laughed it off, the jouncing no-son-of-mine, the wedding. But Janie was serious. She stood there in her pinky room, ninety pounds of nonviolent resistance, and drained her lungs. "I was hoping," she said.

"Oh, lamb," I said. "Don't hope! If you really want to go I'll find the money somehow." I'd fight, steal, kill for Janie, happily, with joy!

She laughed at me. "I was *hoping*, Mum, that you'll wear a dress."

I ran around the corner to pick up groceries for dinner, Orangina for Janie, a bottle of wine for me and those *escargots* I used to buy at the Minimarket—a tin of French garden snails with a row of pink shells stacked on top. They were half price, low on the food chain, and really delicious. Janie never ate real food anyway. I bought them proudly with my food stamps, remembering my old hero, Emma Goldman, who said everybody has a right to beautiful and radiant things.

La Rue, the janitor of our building, was digging a hole in the square foot of garden out front, one eye patched and blind from some disease that would have been preventable with national health insurance. She wore rubber guards strapped around the legs of her blue jeans. She slashed dirt with her shovel and then looked up, as if she'd been waiting for me, and dumped a pot of blue marguerites into the ground. From her dark look I knew she'd been talking to Janie.

"So—she's not in such great shape," La Rue said. "Do you really want to go up in the air?"

"Yep," I said, suddenly definite. La Rue's pessimism was always useful; it brought up my resistance and vitalized our struggles.

"They got a hospital at thirty thousand feet? They got a cardiologist? I shouldn't think so."

I kicked dirt off the sidewalk with the toe of my Chinese cotton slippers. La Rue had a terrible fear of going anywhere, but not us. All spring I'd been hoping Janie's shrink would invite us up to her cottage in Maine for a couple of weeks. I had it all planned. We'd go by bus. I love the bus—there's no being up in the air, and it's the people's ride. But no, Janie's shrink said finally after weeks of dragging her feet, she had a paper to write on the dreams of terminally ill children (thanks, Janie!) and she needed to go up alone.

We'd go almost anywhere. Alabama wasn't at the top of my list, though I thought I wouldn't mind checking out the new South, running down to the city hall, catching a glimpse of the black mayor. It was the aerobics instructor who made me pause. I thought he might depress Janie, who told me on her eighteenth birthday that she'd give her collection of snow globes to be able to disco.

La Rue had always been opposed to every adventure. She'd been against cross-country skiing in Vermont, against mushroom camp in New Hampshire, against summers in Maine, weekends in Truro, Paris in the spring, against Los Angeles and New York, against oysters and *escargots,* against Mexico, against walking on the embankment at night. She was even against analysis, dreamy armchair stuff which Janie got free from the shrink downstairs—although analysis *didn't* work on Janie. She was too nice, not angry enough, La Rue was right about that. Still, if La Rue had her way, Janie would be hooked up to anything the state would pay for: electrocardiograms, thallium stress tests, coronary angiograms, cardiac ultrasounds, Holter monitors, and we'd never get out of town.

I loved La Rue like a sister, her sullen, spare-me-nothing tragic face, the way she moved her lips over a glass before she drank her beer. I loved her *because* her sensibility was wrecked by class struggle and how bourgeois the women's movement turned out to be. She mistrusted the poor, but she had a touching faith in doctors, priests and the FDA. For example, she still thought the biggest, most perfect-looking fruits and vegetables were the best.

She had an apartment in the basement where she kept her husband, a veteran who was too shellshocked to be useful. She mostly left him to his violent memories, and spent her free time in the storage room next to the boiler, where she kept a crushed velvet recliner and a string of African violets under a grow-light among other tenants' old trunks and bicycles, baby cribs and strollers. When she wasn't on her rounds in the building or digging out front, she'd usually be there reading *The Catholic Worker* in the recliner, or studying the side panel on a box of fertilizer. La Rue was my age, forty-five, and like me she'd spent her most brilliant and productive years in our building, so we had not too many secrets from each other.

"Willis is getting married in Birmingham," I finally told her. "Janie wants to go."

She raised one eyebrow, which signified the upper limit of what would surprise her. She heaped a little dirt around the roots of the marguerites with her shovel. I could see this was new information. "That's your son, isn't it?" she said.

"Yep," I said. "I think Janie hopes I'll change my will and leave everything to their brat babies. It's a make-a-wish kind of thing."

"Why don't you? Not for the son, I mean—for Janie."

"The hell I will," I told her. "It's all going to Planned Parenthood and the NAACP."

"But that would be something, wouldn't it, to see your son all grown?"

Elaborate shrug I learned from Dr. Goldman. Godless arrogant shrug. Who could care more than I care, who gave you life? But now I'm off the case, nothing more I can do.

"Is Janie any stronger, does Dr. Goldman think?"

I shrugged. "That's what he thinks." I shrugged again. It felt good.

Goldman—the guy we had on our side instead of God! He'd held Janie's heart in his hands. He was our man, our cause; the whole building—La Rue too—fought for Goldman. I had to have him for Janie the minute I heard his name. We marched on the hospital, our street wrote a hundred letters. The Rebozos on the second floor had a journalist son, who wrote an article for the *Globe* about Janie and me. It ran alongside a pathetic-looking photo of the two of us in Janie's hospital bed, which the Rebozos' son shot with a special lens on his Leica, lying on his back on the linoleum floor to make us look large. After that, even the state couldn't keep Goldman off Janie just because we got food stamps and AFDC.

People understood that kind of trouble. After the article came out, checks and letters came in, which surprised me. Such imagination and faith—sending money to a newspaper—was touching. It was Catholics, mostly, who ponied up, working people, *of course,* said La Rue, herself Catholic, with a roll of her eyes. ("God bless you," I wrote them all in a rash of breathless thank-you notes, in case that's what they wanted to hear.)

But this time, instead of free surgery Dr. Goldman kicked Janie's gurney back through the swinging doors: Sorry, he said. Deflated, we three moved onto a narrow hospital bed, watching the familiar bad news spike up and down on the ECG. The trouble wasn't money. The trouble was Janie. The trouble was electrical and hydraulic, the trouble was everywhere, electrical alternans, modulated atrial parasystole; the timing was off, the pipes irreversibly damaged. Janie had a cultivated indifference to these critiques. (Who likes to hear her faults?) She kept her nose in a magazine while Goldman cupped his surgeon's hands to show us how the valves were *supposed* to work, like tiny parachutes, opening and closing under the pressure of blood. The parachutes were meant to be silky, graceful, tensile, strong. But Janie's parachutes weren't like that. Goldman shrugged—an expensive animal smell rose from his white jacket—her parachutes were tough as old sailboat sails, he said. He folded his hands, drew up the two index fingers against his lip, and I thought, "Here's the church, and here's the steeple . . ." He might have been religiously Jewish, Goldman; I can usually tell, but his personality was submerged.

A funny-awful thing happened while he chatted. The merry beeps of the ECG flattened out suddenly into a nasal squeal—the steady sound of Janie gone. (But there was Janie on the bed, peeling off electrodes, buttoning up her blouse!) Goldman turned to the graph before he looked at Janie, so strong was that impulse in him to trust the machine. Janie saw it, must have seen it, too. She raised the wires up in her fist and said, "Look, Dr. Go—no heart!" He turned around fast—seemed surprised, happy to see her.

What could we do with that, but laugh?

When I came home with the groceries Janie was sitting up in bed. The blue point of her nose looked as sharp as the tip of a pen poised over her new copy of *Mademoiselle*; she was making note of dresses that would knock them dead in Alabama. "This is the kind of a thing," she said, showing me, "unless Debbie invites me to be a bridesmaid. They're wearing peach, which I hate, but still."

"Who's Debbie?" I asked her.

"Mum! She's the *bride*!"

I went into the kitchen, poured out a little of the frascati, sautéed the garlic, chopped the snails and a baguette, mixed in the parsley and scooped it all up with lots of butter into shells. The truth was, Janie wasn't well. She couldn't lie down to sleep or her chest filled with fluid and she woke up drowning. She had to sit up, stand up, sit down. Sometimes at night I'd go climb in next to her in bed and listen to her wheeze. Try to breathe with her, just be a witness. Or we'd get up at any hour, make pancakes and watch old *noir* movies on TV. We watched *Rear Window, Breathless, Shallow Grave,* a hundred soulless erotic thrillers. Janie was supposed to live about five years, but I knew how to keep her interested. There was Janie, the time we pried a little money from her father, gasping up the long skewed leg of the Eiffel Tower; there she was again, in a black velvet jumpsuit, swallowing an oyster in New York. It wasn't some dumb life, in spite of what her father told me once after he took her out for what he called "a proper lunch." He complained that she wasn't "intellectually stimulated enough" because she couldn't add up the bill for a plain hamburger, a glass of milk and his three gin and tonics.

"You've kept her down, you've spoiled her," he complained.

"Spoiled her for what?" I asked him.

"Productive work," he said with a hard-line look, as if he thought I wouldn't get it. I was furious, and after he'd gone I looked up "parlor Bolshevik" in the thesaurus just to see it in black and white. Then, to be scrupulous and fair, I looked up "unproductive" and read: "uncultivated, celibate, menopausal . . ." Me! But I bore no grudges. Anyone can be narrowed down by an adjective or two, and what kind of truth is that?

We'd just sat down to dinner when I heard La Rue on the back stairs gathering empty bottles. A minute later she knocked and came in with a little box wrapped up with a lavender ribbon like the ones she tied around the pots of her African violets in the basement. "A little something for your trip," she told Janie. "It's nothing much." She shrugged in the doorway, apologetic, but urgent in a way I understood as having to do with life and death, which aren't, after all, simple. Fifteen years ago I cheered La Rue on at the clinic when she had her D and C—the last chance, it turned out, though she never complained.

"Join us for a little wine, La Rue? A plate of snails?" I asked her.

"I poison snails, dearie—but I'd take a drink."

I poured wine for La Rue and me while Janie opened the box and pulled out a light gold-plated cross on a chain—she'd always wanted one. "It's beautiful, La Rue, perfect," Janie told her, beaming. "Help me put it on?" La Rue pulled a pair of half glasses out of the pocket of her denim shirt, but the patch on one eye combined with the middle-aged difficulty of seeing small, definite things. Finally Janie had to reach around and hook the clasp by feel. She ran into the bathroom to examine her new charm, then all through dinner she kept touching it, pressing the metal between her thumb and a finger.

"I hope you don't mind—the cross," La Rue said, pointing to the one at her own throat.

"Not at all," I told her. "Why should I?"

Only I did mind, a little. Later I found Janie kneeling on the floor in her bedroom, her hands pressed into a steeple against her old Winnie the Pooh sheets. God, that kid loved to pray.

*

Janie had never met her half brother; I hadn't seen him myself since before she was born, somewhere over eighteen years. His father sent pictures every Christmas when Willis was growing up, cheesy photo postcards with Christmas trees and glass balls printed on, of Willis and the other children sprung from Freddy's happy union with his second wife. The new wife was a beauty queen from an old southern family, but their children all looked like Freddy, and every year they had more. In the pictures I barely recognized the child who'd passed through me, the red protesting baby on the Chux pad between my legs at the end of a short cord, the tiny Willis I signed up for the Friends' School that same day and took to see the black ballet when he was two years old. (I had hopes and fears for the world, like any married girl of twenty. Even as Freddy and I punched and screamed at each other in our cubicle of married housing overlooking the river, we believed good things would happen to us.)

Children were marching on Birmingham when my water broke—that's what really woke me up. Outraged, I pushed a baby out of me, a picture in my mind of those cops with their nightsticks, beating six-year-old children, arresting them and putting them in jail! Unfortunately it turned out Freddy wasn't political at all. His father was an important white figure in the civil rights movement, a Presbyterian minister who later walked the whole way from Selma to Montgomery. He was the one I wanted to sleep with, but I married Freddy, already a compromise. Freddy's loyalties were all with his mother, who canned peaches while his father turned the world. Freddy was so close to his mother, in fact, that when he left me he took Willis (then seven) back to Alabama. I stayed in Cambridge, "carrying on" (as Freddy put it) with Janie's future father. And carry on I did—at last, thank God! But I *did* send a book a week to Willis, beautiful illustrated editions of *Pinocchio, Grimm's Fairy Tales, Alice in Wonderland.* Freddy's wife threw that one away, he told me later. Which explained why I never got a thank-you note. She threw *Alice in Wonderland* away! Why? Because Willis was a boy.

There was no word either after Janie was born, when for three weeks she lay in an incubator while we waited to see if she would get big enough for heart surgery. "Well," Freddy told me later, "what did you expect? Beth was having a baby too, you know, and at that time Billy was away at football camp."

"Football camp! At seven years old! And don't call him Billy," I told Freddy, not unreasonably, since Willis was his name.

"Mary, every morning when I wake up I thank God that I didn't let you turn my son into some ballet-dancing faggot named Willis," he said.

I called names into the telephone: Bigot! Homophobe! Republican! Nothing would offend him anymore. The last thing he said to me was, "I've got to go, Mary. We'll pray for your little girl."

I handed out digoxin like cough drops for a cold, but still Janie turned blue and wheezed, and had to spend the weekend on the ventilator at Mass General wearing La Rue's cross and a gray sweatshirt from the college she was supposed to go to. I asked Dr. Goldman about Alabama. Was it wise? Would she make it? He lifted his shoulders—he stopped just short of a shrug. He asked Janie herself, "How important is it?"

She was white as paper, her lips were cracked and white

around the edges. She smiled at her doctor, and I thought I heard her face tear apart.

Freddy took me to a bar downtown for martinis the night he announced he was leaving me, and taking Willis with him, "home" to Alabama. He told me fiercely that they were going to be "happy." He paid for the drinks and overtipped the bartender; it gave him pleasure to own the moment.

"You're leaving me because you want to be happy?" I asked him.

"Don't try to manipulate me," he said. "I work all the time while you carry on with that fag-ass guitar-playing *communist*?" His eyes lit up. "I *fed* you," he said.

These are the kinds of words that stay with you.

On the drive home he was so exercised I'd found someone else who'd sleep with me that he grazed a duck on Arlington Street. "Jesus! Look what you made me do!" He yelled and carried on. I climbed out of the car, picked up the duck and wrapped it tightly in my coat so it couldn't nip me, and held it in my lap the whole way home. I guess he thought I'd put it in a box and nurse it with a mother's love. But the minute we got upstairs and he paid the babysitter I hit it on the head with a claw hammer, pulled out the oily feathers with a strawberry huller, and roasted it on a rack with his favorite rough-cut marmalade. He was horrified, but I told him, "You have to eat what you kill." And he did—with asparagus. He always trusted me that way.

Janie's father at least veered to the left. We were inflamed together by folk music and class struggle, but he had no eyes, no aesthetic judgment at all, and he was a snob, I know, because when Janie was born he said her heart was my fault because his genes were good and I was adopted.

I never hated men, but what I loved best were those beautiful early years of the women's movement, when Ruthie Sargent and I turned our husbands into anecdotes, a simple, harmless pleasure that wasn't so harmless that we didn't still enjoy it. Deconstruction was more meaningful for us even than marriage and divorce.

Even in the busiest years when the women on our street were getting remarried, having more children, we were still political, marching on the Pentagon, marching on Harvard Yard. I remember drinking gin and tonics with Ruthie Sargent on the porch of her little house on Hilliard Street one muggy summer afternoon when Ellsberg or someone was hiding out across the street. Janie, who looked six no matter what her age, kept offering the Secret Service men glasses of ice water, three steaming men in suits. It wouldn't have been "nice" to explain why she shouldn't.

We were always planning to take a year, Ruthie and I, and read Emma Goldman and the rest of *Das Kapital.* But then Ruthie left her two girls in Brookline and moved to California to live among women in a warmer climate. And by the time I was thirty-five I'd lost interest in what most men (besides Dr. Goldman) had to say. Janie was my research and my profession, all my success. Money dribbled in, not enough for a bank account or a car, but what did we care? We had no future—we were free. I had regular intercourse with the state, which is how I described it to La Rue, who was deeply, compulsively on the side of the screwed. But even she liked me better when I was married and had cash money.

"Intercourse with the state is just what it sounds like!" I told her. She held her weed-eater in a rather militant way, and said, "So what does it sound like to *you*?"

For years I'd promised La Rue that we'd get together one

night a week and listen to Marx, Howard Zinn, Zora Neale Hurston on tape. I thought we'd do it in winter, have a little bourbon in those long afternoons when it gets dark at three forty-five. La Rue always said, "Any time you're ready, dearie." The trouble was, she had her bad eye covered up with a patch, and without that depth it was hard to read. I saw it all, winter, La Rue and me with the Books on Tape, our feet up on the couch and ice melting down in the Picardie tumblers. Janie was never in that picture, though.

La Rue loaned us $500 for the plane and the motel. I could have asked Janie's shrink for money, but she'd already offered a silk suit and let's face it, where cash is concerned it's easier to ask of the poor than of the rich.

Janie loved packing, going away. "Listen," she said. "I've got it all arranged. We take the noon flight from Logan to Birmingham. We stop in New York, but don't change planes. We can get a taxi from the airport to the motel—maybe we could even get a bus. That's where the dinner is, at the motel—Freddy's paying—and we can just spend the night and get a ride with somebody the next day to the church. The wedding's at two, and I have us on a night flight home."

A week in advance our little suitcase was gorged with our best stuff for two days and a night in Alabama: Janie's shrink's silk suit and Janie's new electric blue outfit, special ordered, size 0, and delivered to Filene's, and a beautiful pigskin case we scored at the Ladies' Aid and stuffed with digoxin, vasodilators, diuretics, lip gloss and Janie's atomizer of Evian water. We did everything fast, ran over to Shreve's and bought an ice bucket, a tin beauty, I thought, cheap at $39.50.

*

I took two Valiums before we left for the airport. We rode the Red Line to the hospital, where we picked up a letter from Dr. Goldman for use in an emergency, and Janie got ventilated. Dr. Goldman was out of town (sailing in Maine) and a nurse we didn't know insisted that Janie sign forms checking herself out of the hospital with heart failure. I carried the suitcase and my grass bag from Africa; Janie carried the ice bucket in the Shreve's bag. Maybe the Valium made people seem more liquid than they were, but I'd never seen so many gone geese airing themselves around the purlieus of Mass General. A woman with a bulging stomach and a surgical mask passed us on the sidewalk, leaning on a three-footed cane. Another woman in a wheelchair rolled by in the other direction; a prosthetic arm hung down from a clamp of stainless steel behind her. An intern in a lichen-colored jumpsuit stood staring up into an acacia tree; he had a tipping table stuck in his breast pocket; he was crying. It seemed pointless for Janie to see all this. The morning was bright and hot, and when I dug into my purse I found I'd left my sunglasses at home. "Take mine, Mum," Janie said, handing over her Ray-Bans, but I waved her off. "Don't be so nice," I said. "You're the sick one!"

A human smell rose from the banks of the Charles, stirred up by the wakes of the sightseeing boats. The red CITGO sign out at the Fenway rose up behind the Red Line crossing the Longfellow Bridge. Red, red . . . I heard Janie's heart beating in my ears, and I thought of a little drawing she'd made for me when she was about six, all red and blue. "A month is a crinkly red circle," she told me then. "A year is a fat blue stick." We got on the Red Line at Charles Street, then changed trains — Blue Line to the airport. We made it up the escalator and onto the shuttle bus. At the curb in front of our airline I checked our suitcase and asked for a wheelchair. Janie had turned gray from walking. She sat on a bench beside the revolving door, wheezing in the shade.

The skycap brought me the chair. "It's not for me, it's for her!" I told him, and waved him on to Janie. He looked at me as if I were all off balance. "You want that little girl to push you?" he said.

I helped her into the chair. She held the Shreve's bag in her lap, and I rolled her around, looking for the elevator. We went around the metal detector—no one stopped us—and found our gate. I saw the plane through the window, behind the woman at her station who asked to see my driver's license. It looked too heavy to fly.

"A credit card with a photo on it . . . some ID . . ."

No credit card . . . too poor. No driver's license, bad reflexes . . .

But she wanted some proof. I remembered Dr. Goldman's letter, and pulled it out of my grass bag to show her. Janie looked pretty much as described. Her eyes were closed, and her head hung loosely over one shoulder. Blue veins ran across her eyelids, and behind the gold cross at her neck I saw the pulse across her sternum move cartilage and bone. "Is there a good cardiologist on the plane?" I asked the woman at the desk, but she was busy typing on the machine in front of her.

"Lucky you," she said. "I can bump you up to first class. These will be your boarding cards. Now go. Go!"

Janie's eyes opened obediently: now go-go. "Thanks for all your trouble," she said.

I rolled her down the chute to the plane and into first class. "You take the window," she said, and I'd sat down before I realized she'd offered me the window because she would have liked to look out. But by then she was too exhausted to move. I could see right through her skin, and her breathing was terrible. She sat there for a minute with her hand on her throat. Then she smiled, pulled a copy of *Mademoiselle* from nowhere and started reading an article on Princess Diana's bulimia.

Before we'd even taken off the flight attendant came around with magazines and champagne on a tray.

"Do you have *Vogue*?" Janie asked.

"I'll look."

"And two glasses of champagne," I told her.

The flight attendant looked at Janie. "She doesn't drink," I said.

She handed over a magazine and I gave her a copy of Dr. Goldman's letter. "This is very important," I told her. "We need to find out if there's a doctor on the plane in case anything goes wrong."

"I'll try to find out," she said. "Did you talk to anyone at the airline?"

"Isn't this an airline?" I said.

Janie said, "Drink your champagne, Mum."

The flight attendant folded up the letter and started walking toward the front as the plane began to move.

"Tell the pilot!" I called after her.

"First class is so great," Janie said. "Lookit, free headphones!"

"Did you take your dig, darling?" I asked her.

She nodded, but took her pillbox out of the pocket of her dress and popped a digoxin into her mouth. "Sip of your champagne?" she said, and reached over and washed the pill down.

The plane went up fast, then hung in the air. I looked

down once and saw the familiar red CITGO sign and the black river crowded with scullers from the Ivy League, striving at their oars. Then the city disappeared. The flight attendant stood in the aisle, breathing through an oxygen mask and the pilot came on over the loudspeaker and said that we might be late into Birmingham; the wind was blowing against us.

The Sugar-Tit

OF COURSE she was furious: while the beef roast browned in the oven she scrubbed the grandfather clock with steel wool and wax. She scrubbed the collars of her husband's shirts and ironed them for the Ladies' Aid. Then she walked up the hill to her father's apartment with the roast on a plate under silver paper.

He didn't answer when she rang the bell. He couldn't go far, he was nearly blind; twice he'd been struck by buses, and survived. Giddy Shortall walked across Beacon Street to the Athenaeum and asked there. Yes, Mr. Wentworth was in with the periodicals.

She left the roast with the man in the vestibule and found her father in a polished red chair. He could no longer make out words, but he was a man of habits and liked to hold some reading in his hands. She knelt by his chair and whispered, to preserve the silence of the room, "I've come with a beef roast." Mr. Wentworth looked at her as if she were insane and said, "Surely you know better than to come to the Athenaeum with a roast."

She led him across the street and took him up in the elevator to his twin rooms at the old Bellevue. She carved off a corner of the meat for him, and filled a tiny etched glass with the juices. Then she read aloud from a novel by his favorite author, Thackeray, scenes of imprudent love and impatient heirs. He would bend and write a check, she knew: his milky eyes watered as he drank and ate. But her father's imagination was more modest than Jack's and his checks were always too small.

Jack was not a suitable husband, Giddy's father pronounced early on. He was an *enthusiast,* meaning he wasn't serious, and Giddy was a fool. But she had married for love, not money, and she remained loyal and rigid in her devotion while Jack's attentions drifted. Now he had an interest in a bottling company in Natick; now he was shipping off crayons to the children of the English. But years passed and the more Jack stumbled and failed at business, and drank, and looked to other women for sympathy, the more Giddy's father came to believe that his son-in-law was marked by a noble and aristocratic heart—an almost Grecian flaw. As Mr. Wentworth grew old this conviction hardened and refined itself until, toward the end, he seemed to prefer Jack to Giddy. It became easier then to ask him for money.

She found his checkbook among the piles of papers on his desk. "Don't go near my things!" he shouted. But she paid no attention and laid a check on his blotter with a pen and told him sternly, "This is money owing to Paula Blodgett." Imagine, owing money to Paula! Mr. Wentworth lifted the pen and licked his lips. His old hand shook as he wrote.

On her way home she stopped to sit in the Public Garden, something she rarely did, though she lived just around the corner. Her legs still hung down from the bench: she wasn't five feet tall, a tiny person forty years of age. Spread out before her the Garden seemed brilliant, the new leaves luminous under the gray branches of the trees, a grid of tulips sprung up in the freezing air. There was the familiar ginko tree with its button knobs, Oriental and severe.

She had sat on this bench when she was a little girl, waiting for her mother and her father to come and get her after Symphony. Every Friday afternoon she followed them through the Common and into the Public Garden, two gray suits of worsted sliced from the same bolt. It was always winter during Symphony, brown sticks for trees after the leaves fell off, the sky a dull penciled gray. Wind blew through her gray wool coat, but there was nothing to do but wait: they told her to. Her father pointed with his stick to this bench and she sat down. Her legs hung above the walk. "Don't budge from this spot until we return," he told her, and Giddy, obedient, never moved. Her mother and father went to hear *Messiah,* but there was no question of Giddy going into Symphony Hall. She had asthma: she might wheeze.

(Jack never believed a word of it. "Impossible!" he told her. "You would have been plucked up by the white slavers!" But no, she remembered her father's expression of rapture, as he crossed the park. She had always felt perfectly safe in the Public Garden. You were then.)

Jack was dead. She still saw him vividly, however, enormous and enthusiastic after one of the Blodgetts' lunch parties, full of wine and gin and desperate to leave Paula Blodgett with a crush. The terrible vision rose up before her eyes. Jack broke away from the group in their camel hair and furs, ran away down the path and up to a policeman who stood at the edge of the Swan Boat pond. The policeman took a step forward in greeting; the black brim of his cap nodded up and down. Laughter blew through the thin air, laughter and Paula's voice calling "Jack, Jack!"—laughing, encouraging him. Jack put out his arms and lifted the policeman up, kissed him on the mouth, embraced him! He would do anything to make Paula laugh. (Paula held her face in her hands and roared.) The policeman hung for a moment in Jack's arms and put two fingers to his lips. Then he seemed to lose his balance, and stepped backward; one foot sank into the ice water of the pond. The Blodgetts and some of their guests pulled him out immediately and surrounded him.

Giddy slid forward on the bench until her feet touched ground. Light glinted off the gold rims of Jack's glasses and flashed as he moved toward her, his hands out like a beggar's. He seemed happy to see her. She walked toward him, unlatching the knob of her fishing creel, and handed him her handkerchief, which was still moist from the Blodgetts' gin. "You'd better blow your nose," she said.

A police car pulled up to the Arlington Street gate. The party of men and women put the policeman into the passenger seat, and he was driven away. Even Ned Blodgett said there was no harm done.

Giddy dressed carefully for lunch at the Blodgetts. The last time she'd worn a brown worsted suit and a string of cultured pearls. Paula was quite bohemian herself, she was a free spirit; but she was also an imperial person who would cut you dead if you weren't correct.

Giddy presented herself to Jack in the kitchen. Was a baby blue scarf at her throat too much? Yes, he said, it was. She flung off the scarf with all her force, but it drifted and landed in a bowl of pippin apples. "Everyone adores you, darling, you're perfect," Jack assured her, smiling. He kneeled on the floor in front of her while she tied a tight bow around his neck. He was over six feet tall, a giant. Adore her? He adored her: the way the iron ramrod of her will butted up against the fortress of her reserve. The sweaters she knit for him turned out too tight, or the sleeves too long. He wore them everywhere: he adored her. But it was Paula he loved. When Giddy finished with his bow tie, she tugged the loops and slapped him on the shoulder. She was always rather physical, rather violent, with him.

Jack stood up and smashed his head on the doorjamb. She saw him bleeding, waving her away, making her look. She mopped his temple with a piece of an old nightgown from her ragbag. These rooms were too small for him. It was like a Dutch house, every room on a different floor. It was old and charming. (But for him it was crowded and tight!) Jack's arms hung down at his sides, the woolly cuffs of his sweater covering the backs of his hands. He seemed indifferent to his wound, cocked his head away from Giddy's Band-Aid and her swabbing hand.

"Stop bleeding!" she told him. "We'll be late!"

They were already late. Two men from Skinner had just left with her mother's tambour desk. At noon Giddy was still pulling treasures from the secret drawers—letters, stamps, her son's report cards from school. Two men came and wrapped the desk in a quilted silver pad, lifted it up and took it out. But it wasn't enough—one desk. Jack needed an enormous amount of money for his business. He needed a ship—a ship—to carry all the crayons he would send to the children of England. Even as she stuck a Band-Aid on his forehead she saw him looking cagily through the door to the dining room, assessing the red Sarouk. He blew his nose into a dingy-looking handkerchief. "Here," said Giddy, and he put it in her hand.

He held out her coat, and she backed into it, struggling with the tight sleeves, then the globular buttons. She followed him out. He didn't bother with an overcoat; he lived to suffer. Above him outdoors rose the old ailanthus, her favorite tree, tall and erect; it had—she had read this somewhere—a *handsome habit.* Most of the ailanthuses had been chopped down years ago because their blossoms stank and fouled the old cisterns on the roofs. But it turned out the flowers of the female had no scent; the rankness was in the male.

Under the tree she reached up and touched his forehead where an orange stain of mercurochrome had spread outside the confines of the bandage. "They'll think you got drunk and fell down," she told him. Her fears—what people would think—amused him. He smiled and rose above her.

"Maybe I *will* get drunk and fall down," he said.

They walked uphill. It was spring, still bitterly cold. One side of the street bloomed with magnolias, pink tongues and gray branches against the bricks. Forsythia, pussy willows—Giddy loved the look of flowers without leaves, something lush growing on a stick.

Paula and Ned Blodgett lived in a rosy brick building with a modest bow front and a few old lavender panes. Giddy saw right away that her own costume was too prim; Paula wore a Chinese pajama in red and purple mixed with other colors. She carried a drink in her hand and greeted her guests with a worldly, croupy laugh.

Giddy and Jack had to climb a flight of stairs and put their coats down on a bed. Bill Dooling was there smoking and Paula said in her imperial voice, "Put out your cigarette, please, Bill. This is my bedroom!" It was a bold thing to say, but Paula was very bold. Her people were loyalists who fled to Maine in the Revolution: they wanted a king. Giddy could hear it in Paula's voice when she said "my bedroom!" She gave out favors, took what she wanted; she talked like a king.

They drank cocktails in a room filled with charming antiquities from Salem and prizes from the East Indies and hundreds of Greek things. On the mantel an urn showed Zeus about to carry off Ganymede. Swords poked out of the umbrella stand, and there was an old piano with unusually wide keys, which had belonged to some famous big-handed pianist. Giddy's friends towered above her, their bosoms wrapped in loopy Irish tweeds thick as bathmats, or in woolly sweaters. They talked about where the best pies came from—Brookline. Plasticene deviled eggs bobbed on the ends of their fingers, crystal triangles of gin bobbed in the air. The room shuddered with laughter.

Giddy rubbed her suit with a handkerchief—gin had rained down the side of someone's glass—and released a whiff of napthalene from the mothballs she kept in her pockets. She stuffed the wadded cloth into her little wicker fishing creel. The creel was not proper or correct, but Giddy was devoted to it. Jack had brought it back from England and it had her initials embroidered in yarn above the clasp.

Jack drifted away from her and landed near a low table of canapés, deviled eggs, stuffed celery and olives. His liquid tenor rode above the rest of the men's voices, in the quivery way of oil on water. He went on about the crayon business—why did he go on? No one asked to hear it—about all the pigments and vats, the problem of shipping, about the ship that would take the crayons to the little children in England. Giddy sipped her drink and listened to him become enthusiastic, to the high sound of his implacable happiness. (Did it sound to Paula like happiness?) There he was in a circle of men, his face rosy and his blue eyes hard; his glasses glittered. He pulled out his handkerchief and honked into it.

Since she could remember, Giddy had washed out handkerchiefs full of stuff from men's noses. First her father's nose, then Jack's.

He stood in front of the fireplace turning Paula's Greek urn in his hands in such a casual way that Giddy was afraid he might drop it. He laughed; a beaming hot happiness came off him. "What do you make of this, darling?" he asked her.

She pinched the sleeve of his sweater in her fingers.

"Two cocktails is plenty," she told him.

He looked at her tragically, to remind her (she supposed) that he was a tragic man, a failure in business, and unfaithful; none of his passions were perfectly requited, and Giddy would never understand him. "Two is not enough!" he said. He held the urn uncertainly.

"Here," Giddy told him, and he put it in her hand.

He spotted Martha Sargent sitting on a needlepoint chair with her yarn bag, drinking a martini and casting on for a sleeve. "Women spinning out the threads of fate—terrifying!" he called to her.

"Terrifying for *you,* maybe," she told him, jabbing at him with her knitting needle. Giddy sat down. She and Martha talked about their children, Giddy's boy and Martha's girl, Ruth, who went to the same school where Giddy's father had taught—and had led the crusade against admitting girls. Ruth was a rather manly child, very strong and argumentative. Giddy's son was the most decent boy in the school—everyone said so.

Giddy herself had studied at home, except for a few months when she attended a school that met only outdoors, in the fresh air. The school attracted her father, who was transcendental. But Giddy failed to thrive outdoors; she caught pneumonia, and almost died. She never went back, and through what would have been her high school years she had "conversations" with her father. Giddy was his only "pupil" by then. Every morning he read aloud to her from a small Greek book. He interrupted his reading to ask her questions as they came to him. Was the point of architecture to reflect society or reform it? Reflect or reform? Summarize or improve? The library was a populist palace: was that good? The people went. They went indeed! He had himself seen in the Bates Reading Room a woman with a kerchief round her head, reeking of urine from her voluminous skirts, ask for the definitive *Larousse*! The murals by Sargent were very bad, didn't Giddy think so? Or did she adore them? What was the purpose of art? What did she think of love between men?

The school was wickedly expensive, but Giddy insisted that her son go, that he live in a castle at school. He came home weekends—her decent, perfect, beautiful boy. She loved him fiercely, more than she had ever loved anyone.

Jack drew some of the men into the conversation, which veered immediately to the subject of ancient Greece. Ned Blodgett in particular was crazy about Greece; he had studied it with the illustrious So-and-So. Ned was always writing epigrams and variations on Greek themes and firing them off to the men in the mail.

Martha Sargent drew herself up and said it made her furious to hear about the Golden Age of Greece as the height of human achievement, et cetera. "What woman would choose to return to the ancient world?" she asked, with real feeling. No one had an answer. Martha said, "You boys are on your own then!" and went off to help serve lunch.

"Oh, but you are hard and narrow, woman!" Jack called after her.

"Martha's all for the girls, you know," Bill Dooling said.

Jack looked down and seemed delighted to find Giddy there. "But, Giddy," he said. "We live in the Athens of America. Wasn't the Parthenon built by a Harvard man?"

"No!" Giddy told him definitely. She would not let him make a joke of her; but he wouldn't let go. Giddy should know, he insisted—she was keen on architecture. The men turned their attention to her, their benign smiles and pinkish eyes beamed down on her like soft reading lamps. Who built the Parthenon?

"Who then?" Jack pressed her.

She really didn't know. Bulfinch? (They all laughed loudly to show that they were with her. She was charming, she was adorable!) She blamed herself; her father knew all about the buildings. He had books—she could have read them. She hardly remembered the Parthenon, though she and Jack visited Greece, on a ship, before their son was born. She hated Athens: there was a hill there, at the top of the city, but the picture of it that came to Giddy's mind was deficient, only crumbling columns and that visible yellow heat under which the old marble trembled. On the ship Jack claimed to be charmed by her detachment from the oppressive march of ages. "Victorians swooned at Athens!" he cried at the dinner table. "My bride remained unmoved." An extremely tall woman from England, who made trouble by eating only vegetables and called everyone "love," took Giddy aside and told her *sarcasm* was a Greek word. "It means torn apart by dogs, love."

In her berth at night Giddy stared into the oscillating Greek darkness. Was Jack a dog? Would he tear her apart? But then she was sick among all the Cyclades, too sick to wonder, and Jack brought her ginger ale, and made her laugh with a tale of the Englishwoman demanding a fried tomato at Crete.

It was the last time Giddy and Jack traveled together; after that he had only gone to England alone—exploring, he called it. She hardly knew what he did there—he said he sold crayons, which was hard to imagine. He brought them to the schoolrooms of the English children; he told Giddy the children had never seen such crayons, such colors, before. She would like to have gone along, to have seen the children, to have helped him, but business was always going badly and the time was never right. Besides, Jack pointed out, she had their son to take care of, although he spent the week at school.

Of course it turned out the Parthenon was built by a Greek. Jack took the joke as far as he could, and then, when it was too late, Bill Dooling said, "*Stop* it, Jack." He rushed so hard to Giddy's defense, arms and legs flying toward her, that he turned over a candlestand and a luster pitcher smashed. "God, I'm a bull in a china shop," Bill said, and set the table right. Giddy, lowest to the ground, picked up the broken pieces of the pitcher and held them in her fist. Martha Sargent appeared in the doorway with a ham.

Giddy carried the remains of the pitcher into the kitchen. She held the pieces up to Paula, who was talking to a woman in woolly clothing who had left her husband to study at the

Divinity School. "I liked the one in the—sordid trousers," the woman was saying. "I liked *him* very much." Their eyes were wet with laughter.

"We had an accident," Giddy said, but Paula hardly looked down. She just reached out her hand, her fingers banded with platinum. "Don't worry about it, dear," she said, as if Giddy had broken the pitcher, as if Giddy were careless!

Paula leaned into the woolly woman, laughing, the broken shards of the luster pitcher jutting out from between her fingers in their jewels. "You want to put him in a bath and bathe him," Paula said. Giddy opened her mouth to speak, but there was nothing to add. They liked a man in sordid trousers, that was all. They wanted to put him in a bath and bathe him.

She ate her lunch on a needlepoint stool beside the piano, her feet splayed out and her knees touching to make a sturdy lap for Paula's Spode plate. Beside her at the piano Bill Dooling thumped away and grunted instead of clearly singing words. He had perfect pitch and a wild style that was almost obscene. His playing rose up around her ears and she heard him say, *I like you, Giddy. I like your eyes. I like your mouth. I like the way you look at me.*

Meaningless words, like the words of a song. Giddy wasn't sure she heard them at all. She finished her lunch and laid the plate carefully on a side table. She removed her inhaler from her fishing creel and misted her lungs.

Jack called over, "Why don't you turn up the heat, Bill?" but instead Bill played some lonely-sounding chords, and looked at Giddy. "What can I give you?" he asked.

"'These Foolish Things,'" she said.

He played that, then "Georgia on My Mind," then "I Might

Be Your Once in a While," then "Your Feet's Too Big." His eyes seemed to contract and grow redder. "You're sad?" she asked him.

He shook his head, his hands spread over the wide keys. "It's that—I've never played so well," he said.

He began to play again, but he didn't sing. Paula called to him from across the room. Finally Bill realized that his playing drowned her out, and he stopped. "What are we doing?" he asked.

"Jack needs you for a small adventure," Paula called over, "and I need you to supervise. He's gone already, quick! I'll meet you downstairs!"

Giddy stood up in alarm. "Bill, I wish you wouldn't egg him on," she said.

But all his melancholy had left him, and he was suddenly full of good nature. "Come on, don't be a dull girl," he said.

They went upstairs to get their coats. Giddy was struggling with her sleeves when Bill Dooling's arms suddenly tightened around her. She felt his large, heavy head on her shoulder, the bone at the tip of his chin bearing down. His hands reached around her waist and held her. "You are an angel," he said, patting her like a puppy. "Really, I never played so well." That was all; he seemed grateful. Then he thumped after her down the stairs.

It was a frigid day and everyone moved quickly. Giddy saw Paula and Jack up ahead. Jack had no overcoat, only his ridiculous knitted sweater; beneath her coat Paula's pajamas drifted around her ankles. As they crossed the street Bill offered his elbow and Giddy hooked her arm around it. Jack called back to Bill, "We're going to play a game!" Bill excused himself from Giddy and ran loyally after Jack.

It was the famous joke Jack and Bill Dooling played on the

maids. They went to a certain house on West Cedar Street and rang the bell. When the maid came to the door they announced that they had come for the settee. "We have come for the settee!" There was no trouble at all. They went in the doorway and when they came out again they had the settee with them, one man at each end of it. The maid held the door open, and watched them walk down the hill, not far, cross the street with the thing between them, and ring another bell. Paula Blodgett followed behind them, one bare hand covering her mouth in a gesture of mild amusement. Jack rang the second bell. "We have come with the settee!" and of course the maid stood aside. The houses were all perfectly different, all stuffed with antiquity, all green walls or white walls or red walls. In went Jack and Bill Dooling with the settee. This was the joke—trust, obedience! How could any harm be done?

Later, Ned Blodgett helped Giddy get Jack the few blocks home, up the steps, into the narrow house. He chatted pleasantly with Giddy as if nothing were the matter. He held Jack up by his shoulder and his arm, and got him upstairs and into bed. Then he left them. But twenty minutes later Jack was back downstairs, surprising Giddy, who leaned over a cookie tin at the kitchen counter, crumbs falling from her mouth. Jack laughed at her and poured gin into a juice glass. "Honestly, Giddy," he said. "I never knew anyone with such a sweet tooth as you. You do love the little sweetie-pie, the sugar-tit. Don't you, darling?"

She hit him with a rolled-up newspaper. "Aren't you ashamed of what you've done? I'm surprised you can bear to let your own son see you," she told him. He looked at her, surprised. Their son was away at school. There was no one to see him but her.

*

She sold off the red Sarouk. The dining room floor looked bare without it; the room sounded hollow at meals. Her son asked about it when he came home from school. "The rug is gone," Giddy told him, "to a museum!"

"Why?" he asked her, and looking into his blank, good-natured face she saw how tractable he would be. She found herself angry with him, barely able to conceal her rage.

"It was two hundred years old—the best of its kind!" she said.

But immediately afterward Jack's business failed, and Paula threw him over. Not for that reason, Giddy felt sure—what did Paula care for Jack's success? He came to Giddy with the news, his thin hair standing up on top of his head. "There!" he told her. "She won't have me anymore. She's thrown me over! That's what you wanted, isn't it?" He was wild, inconsolable, *enthusiastic*—it was true.

Jack failed; he died. She found him in his bed with the pineapple posts when she came home with her shopping. He was covered in blood, horrible—but the moment she shut the door she doubted her eyes. Fortunately her son was away at school. She called Bill Dooling, who knew the mayor and the police. The cause of death was written up as Jack's heart, a natural cause for a man of forty-eight. No one questioned it at all, and though her son took the loss badly, he pitched a perfect game the next afternoon at school. "You can't let your teammates down," she told him. "You'll find they make you sit on the bench."

Jack left a sum of money to Paula in his will; not a great deal of money, but even so, Giddy had to go to her father to get it. It was a terrible humiliation for Paula, who cut Giddy dead at the memorial service and never spoke to her again.

Twa Corbies

Mony a one for him makes mane,
But nane sall ken whar he is gane;
O'er his white banes, when they are bare,
The wind sall blaw for evermair.

—Anonymous, from "The Twa Corbies"

"Oh, murder," said my sister-in-law, who frightens me, passing crackers on a plate. "Crackers *and* cheese. Oh, this is murder. And what extra*ordinary* cheese—"

"It's Kraft mild cheddar from the Lil Peach," I said, to plug her up.

"*Mild* cheddar. Extraordinary how they get the sharpness *out* of it. Of course we all get sharper as we get older, isn't that true?"

Because she laughs, it's clear Gay meant this as a joke.

"I find myself duller as I age," I said.

"Not you, Billy. You have a rapier wit, just like Tad. Isn't that so, Tad?"

My brother Tad chuckled obediently, but he had dropped his burning cigarette on his lap and now smoke rose up around his legs. Tad looked essentially the same as he had in college: handsome, self-indulgent, remote. He wore what looked to be the same blue blazer. But his face was red-spotty and his blue eyes empty.

Gay stood up. "Tad dear, you're on fire," she said. She spoke to Tad as if he were there.

Tad rescued his cigarette and Gay slapped the cushions of his pink stuffed chair with her hands to get the smoke down. He submitted, oblivious. He smoked his cigarette down to the end; he held the end of it close to his lips until the ember fell from the hard pads of his fingers. Since he fell down those narrow stairs at the Blodgetts' Christmas revel (drunk), smoking was the only thing he remembered how to do. He tipped back his chin in two fingers and watched the smoke roll out of his nose. His mind was gone. If you said, "Would you like me to turn up the radio, Tad?" he'd say, "I'd like a cigarette."

I was once a great supporter of the American tobacco farmer myself. It was my only vice, really, apart from starting cocktails a minute earlier every day, like sunset in autumn. Before my bypass five years ago, my anesthesiologist—he had the delightful name of Dr. Puck—said he would like me better as a nonsmoker, and I was coward enough to stop.

"'Once more unto the breach, dear friends, once more!'" Puck cried out as he shot the soporific into my hand, recalling for me the raptures of the battle at Agincourt as I faded, life out of my hands. (I survived.) Still, at night I dream of smoking; I wake up in the morning and wonder if I've given in.

Tad smoldered in his chair; even Gay could not completely put him out. She'd flung so much water on the chair over the years she'd soaked the old feather cushions and they had a burnt-hair smell that reminded me of our mother, Tad's and mine, a suffragette, standing over an iron stove in Syracuse, New York, burning pinfeathers off a chicken.

Gay slapped the cushions down around Tad, then swiveled around to the end table, cut a square of cheese and fit it on a cracker—"Have some of Billy's *mah-velous* cheese, Tad dear." She was dressed in a lounging pajama printed with clubs and spades; balls of bone hugged her back. Tad was busy lighting another cigarette, and she had to hunch absurdly with the cheesed cracker on her palm, and wait for him.

Why, you're nothing but a pack of cards, I thought. She was outrageously thin, decadently voguish or gravely ill.

Tad puffed out smoke and accepted the cracker. Smiling out at us, aware of being quizzed, he took a bite and chewed. "Very good," he said. "Cheese."

My wife, before she died, taught me to pity Tad and be good to Gay, without whom, she pointed out, who would have the heart to take my brother on? I live alone now, but in a vast community of the aged out near the Dedham line. The turnover of condominiums there is thrillingly swift, and the profit margin pays legions of employees to remember residents' names and cheer us on as we flog out our final days at our clubs and dinners and attend each other's funerals, secure in the knowledge that we will never impinge on the patience of our loved ones, as Gay and Tad impinged on mine. Gay, for example, should have unloaded Tad to an asylum years ago, sold her apartment. Now look where we were. She had saved his life, after his drunken fall, and brought him back from the dead. Dr. Wesley had said himself, "If he survives, Tad will be a vegetable all his life." And yet Gay had fought for his life! She spoiled him. Now anyone could see she was in trouble. Last month, leaning into a cupboard for a carton of cigarettes, Gay had tripped and broken three ribs. Days later the postman noticed the box was full and called the authorities. "We were getting hungry here, weren't we, Tad?" Gay—still on her back on the kitchen floor—cackled when the policemen broke in and found her. While Gay lay invalid, Tad sat in his pink chair with his carton of Pall Malls and blew smoke rings in the face of death.

My mission in the city, then, was defensive: I would babysit my brother so Gay could go to the hospital for what she called "a little checkup." Selfishly, I feared for us all. Once Gay was billeted in Mass General, I couldn't imagine who would have the authority to release her.

"Look here, you had better write down the name of your doctor on a pad before you go tomorrow," I said.

Gay laughed hilariously. "Oh, Billy, you wag! So if I don't come home, you're going to come and get me, is that a deal?" Truly, she terrified me.

"I was simply—" I said. Simply what? My fingers ranged in a glass bowl for nuts.

"You were simply concerned. Isn't Billy adorable, Tad?"

In Gay's blue-painted kitchen I dumped the ice and gin at the bottoms of our two glasses into the old metal sink. Gay dumped a jar of preserves over a roast chicken. She poured hollandaise sauce into a gravy boat.

I stepped into the airless dining room, which gave off the peroxide odor of tarnished silver. "Put out your cigarette, Tad," I said, and sat down at the table. He was like a child, a certain petulant obedience I recognized from fifty years of teaching school. Back then I used to keep my own pack of Lucky Strikes on the lectern when I recited in Oral English. Poems, cigarettes.

It is some years now since I was there. The school has admitted girls, who no doubt clamor for Emily Dickinson and the lady suicides. I say, let them go. I say, bring on Shakespeare and *Henry V*! Bring on Walter Savage Landor, Lord Randall and the Twa Corbies. Bring on—in season—Ernest Lawrence Thayer!

"Would you serve the rice, Tad dear?" Gay twittered, and set down a casserole and a spoon before him. Tad picked up a plate and spooned rice onto it. When Gay walked back into the dining room with a basket of rolls, Tad had just transferred the entire casserole to the first dinner plate.

"Tad, what a generous heart you are!" Gay said hilariously. "Shouldn't we give some of the casserole to each person?"

"Have some more rice," Tad said.

"But then, dear, what would be left for you and Billy?" Gay asked. She divided the rice among three plates, her hand spread over Tad's on the spoon.

"I'll have a plate of chocolate ice cream," Tad said.

"The ice cream is for dessert, dear," Gay said. "Look, Tad, I have asparagus too, with hollandaise sauce." Somewhere on the way she had reduced the roast chicken to shreds and strings. She shook some of it onto our three plates and stabbed two spears of asparagus for each of us.

Tad reached into his jacket pocket and pulled out his pack of Pall Malls.

"Darling, we smoke *after* dinner," Gay said.

"Goodnight," Tad said, and stood up.

"Oh, mercy," said Gay. "What are we going to do with you, Tad?" But he was gone.

I had assumed that with Tad out of the way we would

speak soberly about the immediate future. Instead Gay brought down two cut-glass cordial glasses from her sideboard and struggled with a bottle of wine.

"I'm not much of a traveler in the wine world," I confessed. "I would make another martini, with your permission."

"*Would* you, darling Billy?" Gay cried.

I would and did, while Gay talked nonstop. "My aerobics class is perfectly *mah-velous.* Why, we leap and run in place —what a workout, I'm sure! And the women are fascinating! We have a veterinarian and a biologist. Isn't that extraordinary? I told Tad about it—he was so surprised." Her hand, uplifted from a raised elbow throughout this speech, held a fork with a few grains of rice on it. Rice fluttered down off the fork as she spoke until none was left. Then Gay moved the fork into her mouth and went through an act of chewing and swallowing—nothing.

"Simply *mah-velous,*" she said, a lie and a habit, but with a glass of gin in my hand I forgave her. Nothing about her was real.

After dinner she kept talking, sprinkling cigarette ash onto her uneaten chicken. Her arms cut the air like scissors. For years Gay had sold tickets at the Colonial Theatre, where she learned to ape the exaggerated gestures of actresses, and dress like a floozy. Years ago, I recalled, she had written a play, but then Tad had his fall and nothing came of it. Fortunately, none of that came up—Gay's yearnings, her lost life. We went to bed early.

Past midnight I found myself wandering through Gay's rooms in my BVDs and my raincoat, looking for the loo. I turned right instead of left and here were Gay and Tad, cadaverous on their backs under a white sheet. A shadow moved along the wall, and Gay sat up. "Billy, what a delightful surprise. Move your legs, Tad. Billy has come to sit with us. Isn't it just like camping out, sitting up late, talking in the moonlight? Let's have cigarettes," she said.

Tad's eyes opened and I stepped back in horror. The claw feet of a bathtub appeared through an open door across the hall. I made my final statement, a hiss in the porcelain bowl, then slept fitfully on the pallet in Gay's sewing room.

In the morning Gay clattered in the kitchen, absurdly dressed for the hospital in a sleeveless dress and high heels. We each sat over a cup of coffee and a toasted frozen waffle on a plate. Tad smoked through breakfast. I had the sense, as Gay applied red lipstick in the mirror by the door and hooked a powder-blue purse over her bone arm, that I would not see her again.

"How will you get there?" I asked her.

"Silly Billy—on foot!" she said. Then she winked at Tad, and went out.

A clock I couldn't see thumped out seconds. Flung back in his pink easy chair, Tad lit a cigarette. I walked a turn through the kitchen, dining room and living room—a circular pattern that led nowhere. The telephone on a table reminded me that I had not got the name of the doctor from Gay.

I dried the three cups and saucers, the three plates and the silverware from our breakfast, and left everything upside down on the drainboard. I passed the morning supervising Tad's smoking and reading some amusing pieces from the old magazines I had brought along for Gay. My memory is feeble enough that any good reading seems fresh.

At noon I told Tad I'd take him to lunch. He stood up and

pocketed his cigarettes and lighter, and we walked out the door, two old men with as little baggage as when we were boys.

Gay and Tad's apartment stood above some old ice-tossed bricks on Pinckney Street; it reminded me always of Mrs. Lowell's famously disparaging remark about that location— I've forgotten it now. I had thought to take us to my old haunt up by the State House, but remembered in time that it had been supplanted. Confused as always by any change, I was drawn to the traffic and noise of the backside of the Hill. We walked farther than I had planned, into less familiar territory. Sausages hung in the windows of shops, washing hung across alleyways. I saw two men eating raw clams at a pushcart while a third man knelt at their feet, shining shoes —or was that years ago? Tad undulated abreast of me, his blazer sleeve hooked in mine. I pulled him along rather roughly into the thick of the confusion. We came to a blind curve; cars sped around it at forty miles an hour. Tad and I stepped down into the street and waited, our woolen elbows almost touching. A delivery truck blocked our view. I breathed the smells of garlic and sour wine; a pulse sang in my neck.

Tad weighted my arm, pulling me down in. Then, thrillingly close, without a breath of warning, a black sedan rushed by. We were spared; my heart roared life in my ears, but how could I be glad? My life is a shuck, and I did not think of Tad as a life.

I brought us farther out into the street, and for a few moments we were penned in by traffic hurtling at top speed on either side of us. Then I hobbled across without him. It seemed the only sensible thing: without Gay, who would have the heart to take my brother on? He would end up in a home, wild and uncomprehending, not allowed to smoke. For a moment it seemed simple, a rectification of an earlier mistake, Gay's mistake in bringing him back from the dead. The crime would be my own.

Tad, sensing himself alone in the road, reached into his pocket and removed his lighter and a Pall Mall. He stood there, fully alive at the edge of death, smoking a cigarette, and no car came.

No car came and ran him down or pulled him into its path. I closed my eyes in a sort of prayer, and heard no shriek of brakes, no sound of metal on bone. No car came at all. Traffic had stopped suddenly on this well-used route when I put my brother in its path; possibly the traffic light had changed.

"Come along!" I called to him finally, and Tad walked across the street without looking. As we walked along I did not recognize myself, wheezing and aloof, my unfamiliar reflection in the glazed storefronts. But I have not recognized myself for years. Only Tad seemed real; his face, unlit by any sense of danger or betrayal, seemed more familiar than my own. What had I done? Maybe nothing.

I chose a well-lit eatery, and we sat down in a booth. A woman handed us menus tacky with pancake syrup. "I would like a hamburg and a cup of coffee," I told her.

"I would like a plate of chocolate ice cream," Tad said.

"I don't suppose you have the slightest idea what's going on," I said when the woman left.

"No, no," said Tad, pulling his Pall Malls out of his jacket pocket and shaking the pack.

Nothing came out but some tobacco and lint.

"Here, here, let me do that for you," I said. I took his Zippo lighter from him and shook the pack, but nothing fell out. The weight of the Zippo felt familiar in my hand, the metal smooth under the wide blue flame.

Though lunch would be my treat, of course, I would ask Gay to pony up for the cigarettes. At the cash register I pointed to a pack of my old brand under the glass, since they didn't carry Pall Malls. When I returned to our booth Tad already had a cigarette burning in his lips. I recalled Gay telling me how he had become quite cagey, hiding smokes all over himself.

"The usual considerations don't apply to you, do they?" I asked.

"Mmmm-mmm," Tad nodded his head, dragging on his cigarette and watching the smoke drift.

"Tell me, Tad, do you remember the accident at all, falling down the stairs? Do you remember our mother?"

"Where is Gay?" he said, and leaned back while the waitress put a silver dish of ice cream and a spoon in front of him. Tad held his cigarette between two fingers while he ate. When he finished and the waitress came to take the dish away he said, "I'll have some more of that."

"Certainly, sir," she said, and was gone before I could stop her.

The next time Tad asked for more ice cream, I took out my wallet and asked for the bill.

"Do you want the ice cream first?" the woman asked, confused.

"Of course not."

"Good *Lord*," Tad said, and stood up.

Neither of us spoke on the way back. We got across the wild streets safely, no thanks to me, and up the Hill. We climbed the narrow stairs to the apartment. There I left Tad to his own devices and went to my pallet in Gay's sewing room. I lay there looking at relics: a ceremonial sword and scabbard hung on the wall, a portrait of a pretty young woman painted after the manner of Sargent, a tavern table with a lamp and my book on it, a Liberty ragbag beside the low milking stool Gay told me she actually sat on while she darned Tad's socks, and an Oriental rug of such ancient age that it had become partly embedded in the floor. I pictured Gay sitting on the low milking stool, darning socks, her skinny pins splayed out around her.

When I got up an hour later I saw Tad from the corner of my eye, spread out on the chenille bedspread, his brown shoes stuck up like boards on the bed. The ordinariness of the scene surprised me: a conjugal bedroom, Gay's glass and silver jars, a basket of scarves, bottles of eau de cologne and aftershave on the bureau, Tad's blue blazer hung on a valet in one corner.

That night I believe he missed her. "Where is Gay?" he said when he shambled into the living room. I felt a prick of sympathy; sometimes I woke this way myself, needing my wife in some ordinary way and then seeing her again, with the milky blue bubble of morphine on her lip.

"Do you know who I am, Tad?" I asked him, but he would not say.

"Where is Gay? Gay!" he called. He rushed through the place, leaning heavily on Gay's fragile wicker end tables and rotten painted chairs. Finally, he came back into the living room where I was sitting in a rocker, reading and drinking a martini. He stood in the door.

"Gay is at the hospital," I said clearly.

"I'll wait downstairs, then," he said.

A thrill buzzed through me. I gave him *Henry V*, "'Once more unto the breach, dear friends, once more,'" but he remained blank. "The hell with you," I said, and returned to my book.

Instead of leaving, Tad sat down in his chair and pulled out a half-smoked cigarette from under the seat cushion. He faced me boldly, with his head tipped back, looking as if he might laugh or smile, or as if he thought he had one up on me. I mocked him a little, and gave him more of King Henry: "'Now set the teeth, and stretch the nostril wide,/Hold hard the breath, and bend up every spirit/To his full height—" and then found, to my horror, that I had forgotten the rest.

Tad went to bed early—it couldn't have been after six o'clock. I was still reading when he came in an hour later, dressed in his usual costume, and demanded breakfast.

He sat down in his chair and threatened, in the act of lighting a cigarette, to set the upholstery on fire.

It was all too much. I stood up and faced him down, the way we used to play Stink-Eye. "You've been spoiled," I said. "No more!" My voice was loud; it shook. Tad's eyes clouded over, as if he were taking in some terrible news. I felt, not without satisfaction, that I had finally got through to him.

I'd hoped Gay would return before sunset so I could cut out early, but by the time the key scratched in the door the last gasping bus of Frog Pond Village do-gooders had left town for Dedham, and I was a prisoner of the dark. Gay seemed like a body from which the spirit had fled. She moved a vase of vivid plastic flowers from the piano to the cocktail table and flitted like a moth. I imagined her, just as she stood, clinging to a curtain and crumbling into yellow powder. "Did you boys manage? Did you find anything to eat? Oh, Billy, how delightful of you to take Tad out to lunch!" She snatched at my hand and her fingers felt like dust.

When Gay was gone I would list the apartment with Hunneman, send the few good things to auction at Skinner and give the rest to the junkman. At my age I have no interest in Tad's artifacts. I would send Tad to a home.

She brought out the gin bottle and I stirred our martinis in a small flower vase and poured ginger ale for Tad into a jelly glass. "Well, you have been to the doctor," I said, opening the subject—long-term coverage for Tad, the living will, executorship, any unindited wishes of the testatrix.

"Oh, Billy, how good of you to ask. Everything is just fine, thank you." She left me with Tad and bustled over chicken pot pies, which we ate out of their tins off TV trays in the living room. "Shall I turn on the radio?" Gay asked afterward. "Tad just loves music, don't you, Tad?"

My eye had hung since yesterday on the pack of cigarettes I had bought for Tad—my old brand—and the hunger had grown in me until I finally got up and picked up the pack to shake out a smoke and revisit that old haunt one more time. Who would tell me no?

But once again the pack was empty.

Gay took away the TV trays and then tottered back in on her high heels with tiny glasses of gin. "Would you like a cordial, Billy?" she said, handing over a glass, which I accepted though I spoke rather sharply to her. "Before I forget, Gay, I might ask you to make good on this pack I bought for Tad. He's run through it already."

She put down the drinks and rummaged through her purse and then through her wallet and finally extracted two dollar bills and some change.

"Is this enough?"

"That should cover it," I said. I was rather rough on Gay for the rest of the evening, so annoyed with myself for almost smoking, for giving in now when I had not given in before.

I woke from a dream in which I was pinned to Tad's pink chair, smoking cigarette after cigarette and puffing out "The Cremation of Sam McGee" to a roomful of students. I woke guilty on my pallet in Gay's sewing room. My pillow smelled of old smoke. I walked down the hall in darkness to the bath, barefoot, in BVDs and my tan raincoat for a robe. A chain hung down from a burning naked bulb under which Gay stood with her back toward me. She wore a thin nightgown printed over with delphiniums, and the bone bumps on her back rose as she heaved herself up from the chenille bathmat to the window ledge with her arm on the towel bar. Her leg bent in on itself like a chicken wing. The black shadow of her head turned; she straddled the window like a scarecrow.

"Gay! What are you doing?" I said.

She turned and looked at me, all attentive, as if I had asked her to pass a plate.

"Do you need to use the loo, Billy? I'll be right out," she said. With two hands she pulled her legs back in, one at a time, from the ledge. Sounds came forth, like joints popping. Through the fabric of her nightgown, in the harsh light of the bulb, I saw the violent crosshatching of her bones.

She climbed down, obedient. I stood in the doorway, a toothbrush in my raincoat pocket to brush away the taste of ashes. I read the handwritten notice on a glass jar filled with cotton balls: "cotton balls." This reminded me, with a pang, of the women of my generation, the scent of powder, the pleasant weight of their hands on a coat sleeve, how steady one felt with one of them holding on.

Gay slid by me like a card. "Don't kiss me, Billy," she said. "I'm covered in creams."

I saw in the darkness the glow of her face and the white spectral palms she held up to ward me off.

And this was how, having failed to do in my brother, I saved my sister-in-law's life, then brushed my teeth and went to bed. In the morning I went home to more familiar ground and left them as they were.

Girl of Their Dreams

WE USED TO GO UP to the lake every weekend in winter when the ice was thick enough to fish through. My mother would rather go anywhere than camp, anyplace rather than out on the ice, but she was a sport, and sport was what my father wanted. He was up and out before she lifted her head from the special pillow that kept her hair from flattening down at night. She'd sit in the damp flowered chair all morning drinking coffee, and at noon she'd put on her fur coat, handed down from her mother, and we'd walk out across the ice. I was young; she held my hand, and carried her pint of bourbon and a glass in a brown paper bag. "Where else can I wear my fur coat?" she asked to show she had no choice. We walked across the lake, our hands in big mittens, the kind that we kept out there, the oldest and the worst. Underneath the old fur coat she wore the gray sweatshirt she always wore at camp, and her Mikimoto pearls. Her Shalimar drifted up into the frozen air, and froze.

She never trusted the ice, even when it was four feet thick, when the air was zero. The ice, when it froze the lake, was white in places, and opaque, and in other places it was a clear black shot through by white needles, and we knew from swimming in summer how deep the lake was. She kept her eyes down, scuffled across the ice and shrieked *Jesus!* when it cracked or groaned. He always set up his hut toward the middle of the lake and even a little beyond, so it was closer to some of the other camps. You wouldn't think he'd want to put his hut anywhere near the Bostons' cottages on the other side, but in winter there were never any Bostons around, and it was worth the extra trouble to catch their fish.

My father mauled logs and stacked firewood up the side of the camp to the roof. He painted the ice hut every fall and got it ready, dragged it across the lake on the hitch at the back of his truck. He drove it back to shore again before any thaw. When the ice was thick enough for fishing he got up at dawn, filled the back of his truck with firewood, drove across the lake and drilled five or six holes in the ice with his auger. He stoked the stove in the ice hut until it was hot as a sauna in there. A red flag popped up on a spring in the tip-up if a fish bit, but this hardly ever happened. Sometimes he caught a couple of greeny-yellow pickerel, and maybe once a winter pulled a landlocked salmon through the ice. This was his greatest happiness, we knew, although he never showed it, and the question of happiness never entered in. Beauty, happiness, he wouldn't talk about those conditions. He came out from his ice hut for us at noon with a can of beans he'd cooked on the top of the woodstove, or he opened tins of sardines. She poured herself a cocktail and he shaved off some ice for her with his pick. We sat outside, because she was afraid the ice would break under the ice hut and we'd get trapped underwater. She drank her drink and he drank boiled coffee. She leaned against the canvas side of the hut and closed her eyes, put her face up to the sun and called out to me, "Don't go anywhere—ice breaks!"

I went around to all the different camps, which looked the same as ours, boards and battens and little docks over the water, but the flagpoles at the end of the Bostons' docks made a *dong dong* echo that sounded deeper than our flagpole, and called to me. I skated on my mukluks to the muddy edge of the lake until I broke through. Her eyes were closed, but it didn't matter. I wanted him to see me.

He had his lunch with us, but he couldn't wait to get back to fishing. He was the one who loved the ice and hard work, tending tip-ups, cutting wood, sharpening knives, straining the ice off his auger holes with his skimmer and waiting for the fish, but she was cheerful and asked, "Isn't this fun?" She was the one who said the air was gorgeous and pointed out three beautiful things every day (black crows in a white birch, sun on the white canvas sides of the hut, red berries in snow). Later, when she and I walked back to camp I saw tears frozen in her eyes. She lay on the cot in the back room all afternoon doing nothing at all, saying he didn't understand her, her life was a waste. My father came in just before sunset from his day outdoors, and felt her moody vapor in the air. He didn't even take off his coat. He told me, "Your mother's feeling ugly," and went out again with his janitor's broom, swept a path in the woods and poured lime in the pit privy.

Fifteen and sixteen, we were all bad girls, Frenches and Blanchards and Whites and Youngs. Everyone knew our names, including the summer boys; we were the girls of boys' dreams. We knew where to go (to the meadow by the shore path, up to my father's camp), when to move around as much as possible, to slam dance, and when to lie still and accept a boy's body parts in the spirit of a gift. Winters we sat in school, filling up the margins of our math books with beautiful drawings of bongs. Summers we waited tables and got rich. We drank Pouilly-Fuissé and ate lobster rolls after our shifts, still wearing our blue uniforms against the rules, and drew boys to us.

All over Black Island, from June to September, summer boys sawed the air like cicadas, buzzing from everywhere and nowhere, and calling to us. They were dark-haired boys with cowlicks and wrinkled button-down shirts, and instead of boots and jeans they rolled their khaki pants up over their ankles and wore their feet bare. When we hung out at the pier we saw them spooning instant coffee into bottles of Coke and jumping off the end of the pier into the black water in their clothes. Lily French had her car, and one time we picked them up—three of us picked up two of them. We all drove up to my father's camp and went in through a window.

The camp was just two rooms, plywood nailed to studs with nothing insulated. There were a couple of flowered stuffed chairs on a rug that stayed damp all year, and an oil drum vented out as a woodstove. On a shelf over the stove my father had lined up his collection of decoy Gilley ducks, drake mallards and loons that Gilley carved out of wood. They looked as lifelike as the real things, as true in their colors and the shine in their glass eyes. A ladder in the middle of the camp led to a mattress on a fenced-in square of floor, and in the cold room in back was a cot, which smelled of old horsehair and, in the pillow, of perfume. The kitchen was just half of the big room, a copper sink and a half-size propane fridge, and a table with chairs for two.

Just outside was a new board deck that was my mother's

idea before she lost interest in my father's life, a place for chairs and drinks and a view of the lake. My father didn't care about chairs or drinks or views of the lake. He hadn't got around to finishing the deck then, but he'd never leave a thing unfinished. Sanding boards, laying them down even—that was what he did.

I forget the names of summer boys, but I remember how those two looked, sitting in the flowered stuffed chairs in their button-down shirts, comfortable in their bare feet and wet clothes, not knowing where they were. I remember their long fingers rolling joints, the way they laughed when Lily and I peeled off our uniforms and stood in front of them, daring them, how they held out their arms to be unbuttoned and told us how lucky, how lucky they were.

In the morning gnats sparkled up out of the dead logs into the air outside. The boys had vanished down the dirt road. Lily French drove us home in her Falcon. I brushed the taste of boys from my teeth with my finger in the car and spat out the window at the blue forget-me-nots along the road. We stopped in the coffee shop for hot cocoa, whipped cream, pancakes—baby food. We ate everything as if we'd been starved; we could hardly look at each other or speak. But when we got home I knew it showed in our eyes, our wild hearts. Our mothers were angry and slapped our faces, and our fathers were afraid of us.

Buck Burns was the best boy from town, the wildest and best. The first time I went out with him he almost killed us both, pulling out onto the straightaway in a borrowed Mustang in the middle of a drag race, daring the dumb boys in their jacked-up trucks to pull back. The two trucks screamed behind us and drifted sideways toward the little figures lined up to watch on both sides of the road. When Buck pulled out into the middle of the race, the figures scattered like sparks, flying off into the fields around the straightaway. Buck didn't even look back. He reached over and touched the side of my face with his hand. I screamed a little: it felt exactly as if he'd run a knife through my heart.

"Who's crazy?" he asked me.

"We are," I said.

I came home at night, or didn't come home, and saw less of Lily French. My mother left my father and me and moved into a motel in Bucksport. She said she needed to go away by herself and think. I said, Good, go. My father asked her why didn't she go up to camp for a few days if she wanted to be alone, but she just laughed at him. Of course it turned out she had a boyfriend in Bucksport. My father knew it, but he didn't have much to say.

He did what he always did, got up every morning early and went to work. He built houses for a living, or added on rooms to houses already in town, and sometimes he worked on two or three houses at a time. All over town were houses he'd built, proof of how much one person could make with two hands in a lifetime if he never stopped working.

She left at the beginning of October. The days were still like summer, but the leaves had started to turn. She packed a bathing suit in her suitcase. "My motel has a heated pool," she said. "You'll have to come up and swim with me sometime."

"What for?" I asked.

Her eyes were a little glassed over from the drugs she took to be happy. She ruffled in her suitcase and brought up a pink compact of birth control pills. "You should get yourself some of these!" she said. "Sex isn't just for boys."

"Who said it was?" I asked her. I would have liked to get through to her somehow, to tell her, for example, that I was already pregnant, but I was afraid of what she might do—either give up on me and go to Bucksport anyway, or unpack her bags and stay home. I'd been spending most nights at Buck's for about two months. We went out every night, Buck driving 90 or 100 like magic on the straightaway. We drank rum and Coke out on the rocks by the shore path and smoked joints and Marlboros, whatever we wanted. I didn't even go to school anymore.

She wrote the name of her motel on the instructions for the pills. Then she said, "Are you really together, you and Buck, or are you just with him?"

I rolled my eyes.

She smiled in her sad way and played with my hair. "You'll look younger if you wear your hair long," she said. "Your forehead is too low for bangs."

"I'm sixteen!" I told her.

"I know," she said. "But you're hard."

After my mother left we got into some trouble, Buck and I—not because I was pregnant. I'd known about that for a month, and by the time I told Buck I was used to the idea, bored by his questions and embarrassed by his big-hearted tone when he said he'd stand by me. I'd already had an abortion once; Lily French stood by me then. I remember shaking all over. I kept my knee socks on it was so cold at the clinic, and everything that touched me was metal. When I looked up and saw my green socks in those metal stirrups I wondered what my socks were doing there. That's how out of it I was. This time was different—I was going with Buck in a steady way. Not that I wanted a baby, though.

What got us in trouble was taking a day sailer tied up to

the town dock and riding out to one of the islands. We didn't really know what we were doing. When we got to the island the Bostons told us to go away. Buck got mad about it; he wanted to go back and burn their island down. But the boat ran aground on the jetty near the shore path. We jumped out of the boat and ran away, but people recognized us. Or maybe grinding down a boat on the jetty just seemed like something Buck would do.

My father made a deal with the Bostons who owned the boat; he went and talked to them in his calm way. Then he got Buck and me together and said the Bostons wouldn't go to the police if we paid to fix the boat. It was a couple of thousand dollars. Buck was a year older than I was—he was seventeen. But my father talked only to him, as if he were the man. He told Buck he had some work to do up at camp, and he'd pay Buck and me to do it. We could go and stay there for a couple of weeks, chop wood for winter and sand down the deck, clean the camp and get it ready for ice fishing. He seemed almost relieved when I told him about the baby, not surprised at all. He told Buck, "You'll want to think about some real work, son." Then he said, "Until you two settle down we won't tell your mother."

I said, "What are you, afraid she'll come home?"

"Watch your mouth!" my father said.

I don't know if he thought this was a smart idea, sending us up to his fishing camp. I'd been spending most nights up at Buck's place; he had his own unit at the bungalows his parents ran. My father didn't like it—Buck's parents were even crazier than Buck—but he couldn't do anything. My father talked to Buck as if Buck was his son, and shook hands and laughed with him. Buck didn't have a car anymore, and my father drove us up to camp in his truck. He set up a fire in the woodstove, showed us the work he wanted us to do.

My father was glad to be at camp even for half an hour, and I could tell he didn't want to go. After he did, Buck looked around in a wild way and said, "What am I, your prisoner?"

I put my arms around him and said, "Yes." We took off our clothes right there on the old rug and I climbed on top of him.

"Close your eyes when you kiss, you look like a fish," he told me, but I knew enough not to try to please him. I opened my eyes wide and pressed them up to his.

While we stayed at camp Buck and I made improvements. We worked on it, but not the way my father asked us to. Buck cut down the scrub pines that made shade on the deck; I took down my mother's old curtains and threw them out, took up the ratty rug and hung it outside. Overnight the damp got into the rug outdoors and brought up a dead smell of mustard and cigars, but in the morning when we came down the ladder we saw the sun shining on the old fir boards, and even if the rug was wrecked it had been wrecked for years, and the camp was improved.

Buck also killed a deer. We saw her our first morning at camp, browsing in the woods. I found the bullets in the kitchen drawer and Buck oiled up and loaded my father's old shotgun. The second day, when we stepped out onto the deck I saw the doe bend her head to lick her shoulder, and some of her red fur flew off over the lake. She was looking at Buck, still chewing something when he shot her. Her ears stood up like cones.

Buck ran out into the woods in his bare feet with the shotgun in one hand and his knife in the other. He yelled, "Get the hose! Get the saw!" and knelt down beside the deer and cut her throat to let the blood out faster.

I hosed the deer down the way Buck showed me, while her

heart kept pumping blood up through her throat and onto the ground. I ran the hose until the water ran clear.

He cut her open back to front and peeled back the skin. He cut into the red net that held her insides. Killing and gutting the deer was the first time I'd seen him care for anything. The heart was stopped, a red rock. Buck scooped entrails onto the ground. He sawed off the head, feeling with his fingers for a space between knobs on the neck, and it rolled over on the ground, surrounded by a frill of skin and fur. He sent me back into the camp for a big black trash bag to put the head in. He wanted to take it to his father, who stuffed animals sometimes.

We had to tear up a sheet to string the deer between two birch trees. Buck was mad that there wasn't any rope, but otherwise I could see he was proud, killing food for us to eat.

My father came up a couple of days later to check on the camp and bring us clams. You weren't supposed to shoot deer at the lake, and my father was afraid the warden might come by. But he was impressed, too, I could tell, that Buck had done any work at all. Buck promised to cut some steaks for my father and burn the carcass, and my father cheered up and drank a beer with Buck.

"The rug's all rotten out there!" he complained to me.

"It was all rotten in here," I told him.

I steamed the clams while he drank with Buck and told how my mother wouldn't eat venison, not even the parts that taste like beef. She cooked it for him, but she would make a little piece of halibut for herself. He said that was the beginning of the end for the two of them, a husband and a wife eating separate dinners.

"What end?" I asked him. "Are you getting a divorce?"

"Don't be crazy," he said.

"Why not?" I asked him.

"Watch your mouth!" he said. He wiped his hands up and down his face. He turned to Buck and asked him, "What are you going to do with a sixteen-year-old girl who's so fresh?"

"I know what to do with her!" Buck said, a rude remark that thrilled me.

The camp was warm from the woodstove fire and yellow from the lamps. After we ate my father sat in the old flowered chair and looked at his Gilley ducks while he filled his pipe. Clouds of cherry blend drifted up. "Maybe try the paper mill if you want to work, son," he said, which was all his advice about the responsibilities of fatherhood.

Buck laughed. He said, "Yes sir, I guess." He played with his lighter, set the flint up, and kept scratching out a high flame. He pitched back on two legs of his chair with the beer between his legs. The way my father was with Buck, talking about dressing a deer and working—it was like he was imagining what a good man he would have been in a world of boys.

Apart from work, there wasn't much to do at camp, and Buck got bored. He started pointing out things my father should have improved. For example, there was no hot water. But the tar paper on the roof got soft when it absorbed the heat of the sun. He found an old sump pump at a neighbor's camp, which no one used. One day I watched him set the pump on the deck and run hoses down from the roof. He ran one hose from the pump into the lake. That afternoon he sent lake water up to the roof and let it warm up in the sun. Then he pumped it out through another hose while I stood under a nozzle on the deck. "Is it hot?" he yelled out, and I yelled back, "It's warm."

He worked all day on improvements. He added more hose up the side of the camp and ran some hoses into gallon milk jugs. It was hot for November, but not hot enough to spend much time in the lake. I sat on the deck in my bikini bottom and my mother's old gray sweatshirt and watched Buck work. He was so good to look at, so ragged and unbuttoned, he rose right up above any other boys who were clean and scrubbed and grateful. I fluttered the little glass ring I wore so that it flashed in his eyes. "You're blinding me!" he called over, smiling.

"Good," I said. I squeezed a lemon on my hair.

Buck took off his shirt to work. He screwed metal loops around the pipes he'd laid on the roof; he got the pipes from one of the Bostons' camps. After a while I took off my sweatshirt too, and my bathing suit. The air was warm, but thin.

He stopped working and came over to me, put his hand on my stomach. "How's that baby cooking?" he said.

I smiled up toward him, the sun in my eyes.

Buck screwed up his face and aimed a fist at the side of my head so I felt the point of his knuckle in the soft spot above my ear. He smiled. "It better be mine," he said.

"It is!" I told him. For the first time, I saw this naked baby in Buck's arms, and Buck with his hand cupped behind the baby's head. "Do you want it?" I asked.

At first he played around and wouldn't say. He turned the hose of cold water on me and said, "Mine?" Then he turned the hose out into the lake and said, "Or isn't it? Whose baby?" he said. "I wonder." He kept it up, freezing me, until I almost got mad. Then he got mad. He dropped the hose and started walking around back of the camp. I stood up on the deck and couldn't even say his name. I yelled after him, "Do you want it? Do you?"

*

When he sat down beside me naked I felt the same way I did when he drove us out in front of the cars on the straightaway and instead of being smashed and killed, we lived. I felt beyond. My leg moved across Buck's back and I pointed my toes hard, until they hurt. There wasn't anybody else out at the camps, but I felt as if all the camps were eyes and ears, watching us and listening. I don't know if this is love, but touching Buck with my hand was like touching myself. I didn't want a baby, though.

The tops of the scrub pines stabbed at the sun until it went down. I thought about this: One night, after my mother left, my father had a couple of drinks and said that if he could go back he wouldn't mind making a few changes in his life. I said, "What changes?" and he said he wished he had set his fishing camp right up on the lake on stilts, or he wished he had set it closer to the road. If he had set it on the road he could have spent less time plowing snow and more time ice fishing. And if he had set the camp over the lake on stilts, the feel of the lake under him would have reminded him of a boat. He also said he would have lived at camp for the last fifteen years and let my mother have her house and her cocktails and her card club.

"You don't mean that, Daddy," I said.

"Maybe not," he said, and stuffed his pipe.

"What would you have done for sex?" I asked him. He reached out his free hand and slapped me across the face. Then he went back to his pipe, calm as if he'd just changed stations on the radio.

Buck leaned over and pounded my arm. "You thinking I'm going to go and leave you?" he said. I pushed my nose into his chest and said, "Nnn-nnn." The beginnings of a terrible smell were coming off the doe in the woods. It wasn't our fault the days were hot for November, but the smell, now I noticed it, was so terrible it brought tears to my eyes.

He either didn't notice or didn't care. He combed my hair with his fingers.

"Listen, I want to hook up that kerosene heater," he said. "I'm tired of cutting wood."

I breathed in the dead deer. "It's broke, isn't it?" I said. "Anyway, he wants the wood for ice fishing."

"He wants the wood for ice fishing," Buck said in a high voice, copycatting me. "What are you, Daddy's little servant girl? You do anything he tells you? You know what that's called, baby?"

"Don't be an asshole, Buck," I said.

"Don't be an asshole, Buck," he said, copycatting. "You think I'm a prisoner here? You think I can't just walk away?"

I sat up and looked at him. "Who's stopping you?" I said.

He didn't get far with the heater or the wood; he got bored. He worked on the deer, cut a few steaks for the propane fridge, but the meat tasted bitter even before it went bad. We ate some anyway. Animals got into the carcass, and then birds came, and we had to cover the deer up with the old rug until we got around to burning it. The smell of the deer was so strong we couldn't use the shower Buck made out of hoses on the roof. We'd go dip in the lake, which was always freezing, no matter how warm the air. For food we had chips and apples, or canned milk and cereal, or we'd go fishing in my father's little rowboat. We cast out and drifted, trailing fishlines in the water behind us. The white paint I remembered from old summers had peeled off to gray inside the boat where the staves curved up. I noticed it when I kneeled down in the bottom and gave Buck a blowjob while we waited for the perch to bite.

We brought back perch and pollock, not too many or too big. I boiled water and dipped the whole fish in the pot to scald them, then cleaned them, cut off their heads and pan-fried them the way my mother used to. We ate them off saltines.

Sometimes Buck would walk by and bump into me on purpose, and then get mad. "Stop following me around!" he said. "What do you mean, follow you around?" I asked him, but he wouldn't say. Once I was eating a bowl of cornflakes and canned milk in the kitchen and he came in and told me, "Why don't you stop stuffing your face and go get me a Phillips head?"

"Get it yourself," I told him.

He went out and came back in again with my father's toolbox and turned it upside down on the floor. "Poor Daddy's toolbox," he said, and walked off.

Looking at the spilled nails on the floor, all I felt was Buck's tongue in my ear. Even when he wouldn't look at me or talk to me the feeling I got from Buck was so strong I thought I could die of it. I wanted to feel it all the time.

Then one night he went to sleep on the cot in the cold room downstairs. I went in and climbed on top of him, but he pushed me off. He was naked and cold—he didn't care. I put my head down on the pillow beside him. "We don't have to have this baby," I said. "I don't even want it at all."

He didn't say anything and it was too dark to see.

"What did I do, Buck?" I asked him. But he didn't care what I did.

I never believed anything my mother told me. One time, out at camp, she took me out to the spruce bog to see the beaver dams. It was early morning, freezing cold, and we took coffee mugs with us. I would have been about thirteen; my father would have been out at his ice hut already. There wasn't any snow on the ground and the swampy place where the beavers lived was gray and frozen with yellow dead-looking grass still sticking up. All around us tree trunks lay wasted on the ground. The steam from our coffee rose into the air. "You see what they do?" my mother said angrily. "They kill the trees—for nothing, for twigs!" We stepped over the fallen trunks—they looked like big pencils, gnawed at the end to points—and walked over the humpy ground to the dam.

"Mostly the dam is underwater," she said. "Each family builds its own. But you see that one? Those beavers made a mistake, they built wrong. Their hole filled up with water and the babies drowned."

"How do you know?" I asked her, not trusting anything she told me. But she led me by the mitten to the edge of the dam and pointed to the baby beaver frozen in the ice. "Look at this," she said, kicking the sticks around the dam with her foot, her face ugly with disgust. "The bastards!"

I saw I could never trust her—because of that look. It wasn't that she didn't have proof.

My father came to get us on a Sunday. We hadn't done the work he was going to pay us for, but I wanted at least to get rid of the deer. It was still hanging from two trees in the woods, rotten from heat where we'd left it to cure. I had the idea to burn the carcass in the woodstove. Buck didn't stop me; he didn't care what I did.

I got a good fire going—it had to be hot. I got the saw and the ax from out by the woodpile, and tied my gray sweatshirt over my mouth and nose. I untied the sheets that held the deer between the birch trees and watched it fall to the ground with a terrible softness. I used the ax to cut parts small enough to go into the woodstove. Pretty soon I saw I should have built a fire outdoors, next to the deer, but I was afraid to burn down the camp. Some ducks sat on the water half hidden in the cattails at the edge of the bog, watching me carry hunks of bad-smelling meat and bone into the camp with my hands. The camp filled up with black smoke; the door of the stove stuck open on a bone.

Buck sat on the deck in his shorts smoking dope.

When it was finished I couldn't wait to jump into the lake and get clean. I pulled the sweatshirt off my face, pulled off my socks and my dungarees until I just had my bathing suit on. Buck hadn't talked to me all morning. But suddenly there he was, picking up my clothes from the floor, laughing. He danced around me, holding the clothes over his head while I jumped around him, reaching and laughing with him. Then he threw my clothes into the fire.

"Are you crazy?" I said.

He grabbed my wrists and held them in his hands. "I'm crazy," he said. "Aren't you?"

I was sitting on the deck with my bikini on, smoking the rest of Buck's joint, when I heard my father's truck roll down the dirt road to camp and stop, the door slam. Buck was in the lake, naked, swimming away. The camp was full of black smoke, bloody footprints went in and out across the deck, and up the walls outside were the lengths of pipe and hose where Buck had made the shower. My father gave me a look and walked right by, and I saw what I knew already—that I would never be much in his esteem. He looked back once, at the mess around his camp, and laughed, a laugh like a dog's bark. He walked up to the lake as if he planned to walk right into the water with his twills and his wool shirt on, but then he squatted down on his heels and wiped his big hands up and down his face like he was trying to rub feeling back into it. "Buck Burns!" he called out. "Why don't you come out of that lake while I talk to you."

"No sir, no way," Buck yelled back, and kept swimming.

"I'll come to you, then, and take you out by the ears."

Then my father was in the rowboat, the bow pointing straight at Buck swimming hard across the lake. My father faced me, rowing, but all his attention was on Buck behind him. I stood up and yelled, "He won't hurt you, Buck!"

The distance between Buck and the boat got smaller and smaller, until there wasn't any distance at all. My father pulled in the oars and the boat just floated peacefully on the water around Buck. After a couple of minutes Buck climbed up, and my father helped him over the gunwale. The rowboat tipped in the water but stayed upright. It drifted farther out across the lake with Buck and my father in it.

Here's what I did: I climbed into my father's truck and drove off, left them there. I would have driven to California and never come back, but halfway to Bucksport I got picked up for driving without a license.

"Where you going in that bikini, little girl?" the cop asked. He was a young one, a sport, leaning in the window and smiling in such a way that I smiled back, and told him the name of my mother's motel.

Mourning Party

TO THE GUEST, peeking through the curtain of her unit, the grieving at the Burns Bungalows must have looked like a party. Men climbed the hill to the main office with six-packs of beer in each hand. Some looked like young fishermen, whiskered boys with honest eyes, sinewy from their struggles on the ocean; others looked like town fathers, middle-aged. Women carried plates covered with dish towels or long bottles wrapped in paper bags. Children ran wild in the yard, as if they belonged to no one in particular. In the drive-up a police official climbed out of his marked car. He hitched his pants to the lip of his belly, then opened the rear door to the poke and brought out a flowered casserole.

Two young women who'd had children with the dead man years ago still lived at the Bungalows, fanning their flames. One had a ponytail down to her arse and the other had a scarred face; Becky and Melody were the names. Mrs. Oates —a woman in middle years, heavy with history but traveling alone—had met them the night before, by chance, when she brought her ice bucket to fill in the front office. The news had just come by telephone from the manager of the motel in Florida where the dead man had been living, and it was still so fresh and terrible that the ordinary rules of intercourse between guest and host did not apply. The dead man's mother still stood near the telephone, smoke from her cigarette drifting up into a nest of jet-black hair. "Buck won't be back, then, he's dead," she told them all simply. Then she excused herself to go and tell the father.

Apart from a certain fraudulence to the young women's initial expressions of grief, which Mrs. Oates recognized as inexperience, she saw something real in this Becky, this Melody. The situation in the office was—it was bizarre. But Mrs. Oates was drawn to beautiful and terrible things.

She took control of the moment, poured cocktails for Becky and Melody in her unit and listened as they wept and spun out grief. The dead man was their lover and the father of their children (but not the baby). They loved him still; they hadn't seen him at all for seven years.

They reeled off names of people they must call. Mrs. Oates made a list, and helped in that way to organize the mourning party. Becky and Melody used her telephone to notify the town, arranged for everyone to meet the next afternoon at the Burns Bungalows, and urged Mrs. Oates to join them. It was clear they couldn't see themselves and thought a stranger might see something.

Now Mrs. Oates stood in her unit and watched the people arrive. The mourners saw her too, and wondered who she was. As the last of them passed by, the curtain swung down over the rotten jamb like a judgment; then Mrs. Oates appeared in the dirt yard, dressed all in black with a purse on her arm, and a package of corn nuts to chip in.

*

Buck Burns was the dead man's name; his mother and father ran the Bungalows. While the mourners and Mrs. Oates converged in the front office, Mrs. Burns stood in the kitchenette behind, surrounded by bowls of ambrosia and coolers of beer. She wore her dark hair teased and sprayed, tight slacks and a red sweater, and two ropes of pearls around her neck, which a Boston man had used one time to pay his bill. A plate of cream cheese and cherry sandwiches had crashed to the floor in front of her, and the pink triangles looked abused. A dog lay mangy on the linoleum, gnawing on an old deer bone. When Mrs. Burns bent over to pick lint from her slacks, the dog jumped up and wrapped its forelegs around her, drooling from its black lips.

"Git on!" she told it in her muscular voice. She shifted her cigarette to the other corner of her mouth and kicked the dog out of her way. "Git on!"

Mr. Burns came up behind the dog and hooked its collar in his hand. While Mrs. Burns swept crumbs into a piece of the broken plate he took the dog outside and tied it to the metal chair beside the swimming pool, a painted blue hole in the front yard filled with birch leaves and brown water.

When the telephone call came, Buck's dog was already in transit to Maine from Florida; Mr. Burns had had to drive to the airport almost immediately to fetch the animal from cargo claims. His truck broke down, so he took his wife's old Plymouth Fury, which was still jacked up from when Buck first got his license. Buck's dog was old now, just a bristle of black wirehair drugged and fouled in a loaner cage. But on the way home, while Mr. Burns dozed with the car running in the parking lot of the Cheese House, the dog woke and chewed out the upholstery in the back seat. When at last Mr. Burns pulled into the Bungalows the dog ran wheezing down to its old haunts on Second Summer Street and mounted the Greens' Pekingese. The dog also almost killed a cat, and would have, if Mr. Burns hadn't driven downtown in time, and pulled it off.

Now he came back indoors and Mrs. Burns, without turning around, asked him for a corkscrew. In his slow no-thinking way Mr. Burns tried to mount her from behind. She walked away toward the sink, and left him hunched there. "Get off, Buzz," she said. "Where's that wine?"

"It's behind you," he said.

"Oh, my God, you're going to give them Ripple?"

He looked at the bottle and said loudly, "Isn't it wine?"

"I guess; you could piss in a glass, those girls wouldn't know the difference from Blue Nun." She stubbed out her cigarette in a seashell.

Who wouldn't be etherized by the death of a son? The town forgave the Burnses their strangeness. Buck was their only child, and what they'd stayed together for in spite of the violent history between them. But he had left them years ago and gone to Florida, and memories surged and ebbed in them, like tides. Mr. Burns's peacefulness came partly from the Thorazine he took every day, by arrangement with the court officer. Mrs. Burns, who wore a metal plate in her head from where Mr. Burns got her accidentally with his Ruger 10-22 rifle one time, was also a little softer than she used to be.

The mourners from town stood up, or they sat in straight chairs lined up against the paneled walls with bottles of beer in their hands. On the walls above their heads hung Mr. Burns's gallery of animal mounts; he took up taxidermy on Dr. Adenoy's advice after he stopped hunting. Becky ran back and forth between the office and the kitchenette with bottles and plates of food. Most of the time she also carried a year-old baby, not by Buck; it was a fisherman's child.

Mrs. Oates appeared in the door, dressed all in black with a purse hung over her arm, as if she were going out. But she came in. The mourners made her welcome; several people gave her a beer. She sat down in Mr. Burns's office chair on wheels, removed her shoes, crossed her legs in the chair, and right away started to make talk.

She looked the preserved animals over and offered a critical appraisal, which pleased the mourners. "These are bizarre, you know that?" she told them. "But there's a feeling for animals here—a real feeling."

Mr. Burns did have a real feeling for animals killed on Black Island, everyone agreed, and he did a good job of lifting them up from ruined victims of traffic or gunshot into lifelike examples of their species. The mourners showed the guest the gray owl that was Mr. Burns's masterpiece. This raptor had devastated some chickens once; now it hung from a pin on a wall. Mr. Burns had raised the feathers just slightly to give an impression of descent; the talons curved over a live-looking mouse, which was secured to the owl by a wire. Also along the walls were an eight-point stag's head with some of its velvet intact and white rings around its black glass eyes, and a cockatoo Mrs. Burns had taught, as a joke when it was alive, to recite the Lord's Prayer. A few of Mr. Burns's early efforts hung there too, and gave a sense of the development of his art, including a squirrel he had cut down so neatly it looked like a vole.

Buck Burns had lived at the Bungalows all his life until he moved away. Anyone could see they weren't much, a handful of one-room cabins flung down in a clearing of birch woods. Daylight shone in through the knotty pine boards and no-see-ums bred in the spongy window frames. Mr. Burns had built the Bungalows himself before he got too drugged to drive a nail, and the town still held memories of those years when Buck had his parties and the Burnses didn't care who came or what they did.

Warmed by Mrs. Oates's appreciation of everything, the mourners helped themselves to the beer they'd brought, except for Becky and Melody who, on account of Becky's nursing her baby, pressed Mrs. Burns for wine. Their boys—Buck's boys—were eight or nine years old by now, both curly-haired and dirty blond, like Buck. They wore old Sunday suits that looked as if they'd been lifted from the church basket. A little girl came in with them, and soon they all disappeared out back.

Mrs. Oates seemed pleased, with a beer in her hand, to pause and listen to stories of the dead man's life and family. Disaster after disaster spilled out—sunk boats, wrecked cars and the violent married life of Mr. and Mrs. Burns, stories to which even Mrs. Burns contributed enriching details. This was still going on when Burton Martin, a fisherman and the father of the baby Becky was nursing, stood to speak in praise of Buck. "It's way too early, Burton," Becky protested, but Burton insisted that he wanted to speak before everyone got too drunk to listen, and finally the mourners gave him their ears. Even Mr. Burns came in for it, and leaned in his sleepy way on the frame of the door.

The truth was, no one ever spoke of Buck Burns except in praise. He was the treasure of the town, and the stories about him had long before hardened into a kind of poetry, high-flown lines that never changed. But Burton stowed his hands deep in his pockets and tried to tell Buck's life all over again: how Buck was larger than life and dangerous beyond the treachery of rules. How temptations other boys fought off by the strength of their character rushed through him like blood in a vein. But Buck also brought out the loyalty people felt toward the wild things of Black Island: the sour berries on the barrens, the lobsters crawling in the cold ocean, the granite cliffs that cracked boats like eggshells and dropped yellow-slickered fishermen into the water.

Those who loved Buck always felt they were going to save him. One time when Buck rolled a Corvair, Burton breathed his own breath into Buck's mouth for eight minutes before emergency help came—fire engine, police car, the helicopter landing right on the straightaway. Anybody else would have died, but Buck rose up into the air on a stretcher with one thumb up.

When Buck was eighteen an advertising agency swooped down on Black Island and saw in him what the town had always seen. They snatched him up like a mussel off a rock and made Buck into the picture of a workingman with a beer in his hand: a Clammer, a Sardine Packer, a Fisherman with His Dog. Buck Burns was not any of those things, but his face sold more beer than any face ever had. The billboard was still up in Bangor, across the street from the Dairy Freeze, and he used to be on TV too until those commercials got outlawed.

But it was always dangerous to go where Buck went, which Burton learned the time he tried taking a few beers and his own dog out on his lobster boat, and the dog went over on a haul chain and drowned.

No matter what Buck did, Burton said, the town was loyal to him. The time he drove a borrowed car off the end of the wharf and almost wrecked a sailboat he ended up in jail, but the city council bailed him out in a 5–0 vote. And who didn't remember those drag races out by the straightaway? Buck sailed into the dark, past Kartland and Dennis's restaurant at 100 miles an hour, and swallowed them all in his noise. A few men and women hooted and wept, remembering what it was like out there, the fastest and best hours of their lives, and even Mrs. Oates wiped tears from her eyes with the ends of her fingers.

Burton hung his head and said, "At least when he died he took no prisoners, by God." He rattled the pockets of his pants and pulled out some of the lucky trinkets that kept his boat afloat—a shark's tooth, copper-plated ball bearings—and turned them over sadly in his hand.

He went on for half an hour, then it seemed he was done. But instead of sitting down he looked out at the mourners and said, "In memory of how Buck Burns touched us let's reach out our hands to each other."

Touching was hard; it seemed like two minutes before anyone could do it. But finally Mrs. Oates leaned over and clasped Becky's and Melody's hands together until, with their hands stiff in the air, old jealousies seemed to dissolve before the mourners' eyes and both women wept. Other hands, then, touched and twined together, and even Buck's boys came in at the end and stood in the back, the square shoulders of their old-fashioned suits just touching each other for a minute. Mr. and Mrs. Burns stood beside each other through it all, not touching but close enough, their faces cool as stones.

When the touching was over the boys helped themselves to the ambrosia and went outside again. Mrs. Burns turned the subject back to Buck. She lit a cigarette, then squinted through smoke at Mrs. Oates and said, "Ask me what happened to all the money he made."

Mrs. Oates leaned forward on her chair and said, "What?"

Becky pulled up her shirt for the baby and exposed a surprisingly large, ruddy nipple. Her eyes, still wet and red from crying, rolled up.

"He pissed it away, every penny," Mrs. Burns said grandly.

The baby, another boy, attached itself for an instant to the breast, pulled away and looked at Mrs. Burns. Then it climbed down off Becky's lap and crawled over to the cords that ran to the neon sign out front.

"I believe it!" said Mrs. Oates. She rearranged her bare feet in Mr. Burns's chair. "It was the same with me when I won twenty thousand dollars in the lottery. I lived so high I couldn't see the earth. But there's always people hanging on, pulling you down. A month later I was handing over my last fifty to buy a round of beer for the Hell's Angels. That's when I said, No more! I want a simple life and real people!"

"Buck was like that too," said Mrs. Burns, "always giving money away when he had it. People hung on him. It isn't as if he didn't make money shooting those commercials in Miami and the Keys."

Not everyone believed that Buck had pissed away every penny of the money he made from those beer commercials, a hundred thousand or a million, however much it really was. When he lived at home and checks came, Becky and Melody always had ideas—snowmobiles, dope, groceries, trips to the Bangor Mall—and Buck had shared the money freely while it lasted. But then he'd gone to Florida, and whatever happened to the money he made there was a question. Now the future swelled and the fate of his two boys and any other children who turned up hung on the thread of Mrs. Burns's interest, which was hard to gauge. She said those words—*Miami, Keys*—as if she owned them, as if she even knew what Florida was, except a state. She didn't know more than anybody else about what happened to Buck once he stopped sending those postcards of Florida or of himself in a bathing suit, looking oiled, with his name and the name of the agency written on the front, and no return address. These thoughts were some comfort to Becky and Melody, who sat without much hope or expectation, sipping wine.

"You don't have to tell me about Miami," said Mrs. Oates. "You don't know what you've got right here: four seasons and real people!" She looked around, taking them all in.

"I spent a couple of days in Miami when I went to Disney World," said Burton.

Mrs. Oates lifted an eyebrow in surprise. Burton looked like a man who got up every day of his life at four o'clock in the morning and went alone to the water to haul lobster traps. But out of lobsters and scallops he made more money than the superintendent of schools. He took two weeks off a year from fishing and went anywhere he wanted. He'd been to London, England; he'd been skiing at Vail. He'd been to Florida just last winter. He never found Buck, though.

"I don't care two cents for Walt Disney World," said Mrs. Burns. "I've got to settle Buck's estate and collect his cremains. I want to see things he seen—Miami, the Keys, the Dry Tortugas. I'm taking his postcards with me."

The mourners nodded, understanding. The postcards were seven or eight years old. Sometimes she brought them out at a ball game or the grocery store to show. Besides these postcards, nothing had been heard from Buck for seven or eight years until the call came from the manager of the motel he lived in down in Florida. Mrs. Burns didn't say what exactly he died of, if she knew, but no one questioned her. Death coming suddenly at twenty-six seemed for Buck Burns like a natural cause. The mourners assumed he died in the night, of some excessiveness.

Silence enlarged around Mrs. Burns like a bubble, swelled and broke. "You going to bring the ashes home?" Burton finally asked.

"If he wanted to stick around here forever he would've," Mrs. Burns said, then she added with her muscular laugh, "but I might do it anyway, scatter him out over the straightaway."

A few of the men laughed with her. Melody clicked her tongue, stood up and walked off into the kitchenette. In a few seconds she was back with a bottle of wine; she poured some for herself and Becky. Mr. Burns leaned against the door, turning over a bone in his hands. Mrs. Burns captured his blurred face in her gaze, then looked around the room and said, as if in her own defense, "*He* can't leave the state, he's got his parole."

"It's not parole, I'm on medication!" said Mr. Burns in his high voice.

Mrs. Burns turned on him with the full force of her rage. "You think you're free to go as you please? People have a right to know what you are!" she shouted.

The mourners turned to hear. What was a man after he shot his wife on his own front porch, and had to live with her for twenty-two years afterward, medicated to within an inch of unconsciousness? Mrs. Burns didn't say. Her eyes darted back and forth across the faces of the mourners. "And anyone who criticizes Buck for getting cremated, that's just how I want it when I go," she said loudly. "That's just how I want it. No religion! No prayers! Just a sack of soot."

"Amen," said Mr. Burns.

"You want me to help you get your stuff together?" Becky asked her.

"I'm not going on vacation," said Mrs. Burns. "All I want's a nightgown and a change of clothes and those postcards

Buck wrote. That's all." And she went out to her bungalow to get ready.

Mrs. Burns, Mrs. Burns! The mourners shook their heads and explained for the benefit of Mrs. Oates that Buck's mother was raised years ago in the clutch of religion. Instead of school she traveled the windy outer islands with a Bible and pamphlets in her mittens. She learned to count by adding souls. Her mother, an old bulb-eyed Canadian, single-handedly ran the Church of the Nazarene and had Mrs. Burns ride out on the mail boat in every weather. Over time most fishing families embraced the notion of a wrathful God.

Mrs. Burns went to save Mr. Burns on Rockrib Island when they were both fifteen, and she came back pregnant. But even after the Burnses married and settled down and she gave up religion, a residue of her upbringing—her highly developed sense of vengeance—clung. In the years before he shot her, she almost drove Mr. Burns crazy with her pentecostal temper. Making beds and breakfasts at the Bungalows wasn't enough for her. Even Buck in some way wasn't enough.

Mrs. Oates had heard it already. "Yup, a fallen angel," she said. "That's a hard row to hoe."

The mourners just looked at her. Then Dr. Adenoy explained that Mr. Burns didn't look like much now, but years ago he ran the Bungalows, when they were a hunting lodge, almost by himself. Hunters used to come up weekends from Portland or Boston, some of them so ignorant they didn't know to chase a deer that ran gut-shot. Mr. Burns was always good with animals. He could hear deer moo in the woods, smell their musk, spot a scrape in a birch tree twenty feet away. Those Sunday hunters recognized in Mr. Burns both patience and a quickness they didn't have, and he built up the business. Dr. Adenoy recalled Buzz Burns shooting a deer and bleeding it out, skinning and gutting it in twenty minutes. "He'd come back with the carcass still steaming around his shoulders and fry the liver for his breakfast," he said.

Mrs. Burns, on the other hand, was always difficult. She couldn't keep help. She fired the chambermaids if they ever tried to wash the blankets or whatnot. Buck was a sweet boy then. He used to follow her around from bungalow to bungalow, help her sweep them out and make the beds. For years Mr. Burns weathered the storms she kicked up and got the city men in and out in a day and a half with a few steaks from deer he had hung and aged before.

The accident that changed them happened when Buck was six years old. Mr. Burns went out one night in a full moon and didn't come back. About dawn she walked out on the front porch to look for him. He testified in court that he took her for a white-tailed deer, and grazed her skull with one of his lead slugs.

Mrs. Oates put a hand to her heart. "He shot her!" she cried.

Dr. Adenoy shook his head. The jurors understood that a man hunting whitetails with an anticipating mind can see anything he needs to see, antlers in the chokecherry, the white tail in a dish towel, even in his own backyard. That's just how the hunter thinks. The verdict was bad luck for Mrs. Burns: she talked too much in court, unraveled too many ancient arguments, and threw the judge and jury into further sympathy with Mr. Burns. But the incident ate away at her. She filed her own civil case and won the right to keep Mr. Burns medicated for life.

Mrs. Oates laughed frankly and nodded her head.

On medication Mr. Burns was still recognizable, but more simple. He slept seventeen or eighteen hours a day in his workshop with his squirrel skins and foam forms and slabs of wax. No one knew how he breathed, with the chemicals he used to kill the fleas and lice, and the fumes of almonds and formaldehyde. He was forbidden to hunt by the court and Mrs. Burns, although once in a while at night he went out into the woods and shined some deer, just to get a look at them. She wouldn't let Buck go with him.

To their credit, the Burnses tried to protect Buck. They gave him a unit of his own at the Bungalows and mostly let him raise himself. By the time he was seventeen he already had two sons.

Dr. Adenoy delivered the first baby for Becky, then later that night Melody and Buck ended up in the hospital too. They'd gone out for a drive, which ended when Buck skidded off the Star Route and ruined her face with shards of glass. Dr. Adenoy numbed Melody with thirty-six shots of lidocaine and pulled out most of the shards with a needle, and then he diagnosed her condition: three months pregnant.

Melody showed Mrs. Oates where glass still came up in her face from time to time.

Becky remembered how much she wanted Buck to see the baby, naked and stippled with cold, its tiny arms rising straight up in the incubator. But Buck's eyes were covered with bandages and he was unconscious. Becky herself never blamed Melody, but the town blamed them both. Those girls were crazy fools! people said. Mixing with Buck Burns then later acting proud of it, steering strollers all around town as if they were jacked-up cars.

Becky moved into the Bungalows first, then Melody. They took bungalows instead of regular child support, helped in the office and lived like a family, even after Buck left them all and moved to Florida and never sent money again. Business had slacked off in the years since Mr. Burns stopped hunting and the Bungalows had gone downhill. Around the time Becky and Melody settled in, the deer laws changed, and the last of the paying hunters went fishing on the Allagash, or they went up to Greenville, where the blackflies bit like dogs.

The mourners got up to eat the food they'd brought, except for Mrs. Oates, who expressed no interest in moving from her chair. Becky brought her food on a plate and another beer. While the mourners ate, Becky and Melody sat at Mrs. Oates's feet on the floor and listened to the stranger fill in the blanks of the conversation and speculate on the future of the Burnses. They might separate, Mrs. Burns might stay in Florida, remarry; Mrs. Oates knew from her own experience that the loss of a loved one set you free, and work was easy to find down there in restaurants and hotels. Becky and Melody leaned close to hear above the ruckus in the office. Some young men were recounting with the police chief and the doctor certain remarks Buck Burns got off to the police ten years ago, simulating with grinding sounds in their throats the trajectory of doomed cars.

Mrs. Oates let on that she had an insurance settlement from Mr. Oates, who had made a small fortune in the manufacture of a surgical instrument. She could go anywhere she wanted; she was looking for a fresh start and a simple life. She wanted four seasons and real people and she dreamed of opening up a bed and breakfast in a place like this. Melody raised her glass and drank, her eyes narrow, but Becky jumped at it. "Why not here?" she said. "What interest do the Burnses have in keeping up an inn?"

Mrs. Burns appeared in the office with a small pink valise

in one hand. She found Mr. Burns dozing in the doorway and pulled on one of his ears to wake him. He opened his eyes and wiped his face with the back of his hand. "I'm going to see to Buck; you brook it here," she said, and kissed him, leaving a red mark on his cheek.

Mr. Burns and a few of the mourners followed her out, wished her well and watched her climb into her Fury and shoot off. Then she was gone, maybe for good. After she left Burton sat down beside Becky and played with her hair. He said it was too bad no one had put Mrs. Burns to bed or sedated her. Now that she was gone to Florida he had a feeling they would never see her again.

Becky didn't say anything. She undid her ponytail and shook out her hair. Burton combed through the length of it with his knobbed fingers. Mrs. Oates, sopping up cole slaw with a piece of brown bread, said again, as if she'd just thought of it, "The loss of a loved one sets you free."

It was a hopeful note. The mourners looked around the Bungalows, imagining the future. Someone poured drinks from a bottle into paper cups and passed them around.

Mrs. Oates pronounced that the town was sitting on a gold mine—the blueberry barrens, the granite cliffs, the lobsters. "It wouldn't take much to turn this place around," she observed, her eyes moving up and down the walls in a professional way. "You want to get new blood in. Those Arctic Cats, cross-country skiers." She gestured at the gallery of Mr. Burns's taxidermy. "Even these stuffed animals would be a draw if the rooms were clean."

The subject of unclean motels led Mrs. Oates to tell a long story about her rape in Daytona Beach. This led to rougher stories about Buck, which Becky and Melody stuck together in denying. When Melody went out to the kitchen to find another bottle, Mrs. Oates made a crude reference to Melody's scarred face; she turned her head to one side and pulled a wine glass out of her nose.

Fred Green took down the stuffed owl from its pin on the wall and laid it on a space heater, where it burst into flame. The mourners laughed when fire sprayed out onto the wood floor and a blue line rolled across the boards. They put out the flames with bottles of beer. Becky took the stag's head off the wall and leaned it up in a chair behind the front desk. She cocked an imaginary rifle and said, "That you, dear?" Mr. Burns, wherever he was, must have heard the mourners laughing. The walls of the office shook.

Becky drank so much she lost track of her baby until an animal noise drifted in from the yard. She jumped up and ran outside, veering off toward the swimming pool to the pixilated sounds of the yelling baby and the barking dog. Expecting another tragedy, most of the mourners ran after her.

It was hard to tell what had happened or was happening. The baby was near the edge of the concrete swimming pool, piteously yowling—and something had gone wrong with the dog. It was still tied to the chair by the pool where Mr. Burns had left it, but it kept crouching down and jumping back away from the baby, barking and growling, dragging the chair across the concrete and sending the baby closer to the edge. Becky ran between the dog and the baby, and the dog rushed her suddenly and bit her on the hand, shaking its head back and forth and biting down. Becky tore her hand free, her face wild with tears and blood. Her lips peeled back as if she might bite the dog, but instead she cried out and swore, and put her hurt hand in her mouth. With the other hand, she lifted the baby and her shirt in one motion, and got her breast in its mouth. The dog threatened the mourners, straining on its leash and barking.

While Becky held the baby in her arms, sucking on her hurt hand to draw off blood, Dr. Adenoy felt around the baby's body and confirmed that it wasn't punctured. Chief Farnsworth stepped forward, hitched up his pants and said he might cite Becky for neglecting a baby. He told her if she ever did it again he'd see she got her baby taken away from her. Then, as if he'd forgotten that he'd come for the mourning party and not just some domestic dispute, he climbed into his car and drove back downtown without even stopping to get his covered dish. Burton also spoke roughly to Becky. What was the goddamned baby doing out in the dark near the swimming pool? The dog was probably saving it. Becky stood and listened, hiccuping as her sobs wore down, her hand in her mouth, the long baby in her arms, its head up inside her shirt, its mouth sucking hard. She looked at Burton and took him in—the father of this baby. Then she turned and walked off to her bungalow and shut the door.

"I didn't like the look of that," said Mrs. Oates.

"It's her kid," snapped Melody.

"Well, Burton, we ought to go give her some peroxide," said Dr. Adenoy.

"Do I look crazy?" Burton said, but Dr. Adenoy rolled up his sleeves, and the two men went off together toward the Bungalows.

Melody asked the mourners angrily what kind of man Burton was, to talk that way. But her words were slurred, and no one paid attention. Everyone already knew what kind of man Burton was. He was hard-working and decent, except in the matter of Becky and the new baby, and even Becky herself didn't hold that against him. No one said it was easy for

Becky and Melody to raise Buck's boys on their own. Those boys were running wild now in the blue darkness, playing an old game called Bear in the Woods, chasing each other and waving a board stuck through with a nail.

The dog never settled down or showed any remorse. It yowled and whined and threatened the mourners, dragging the chair it was tied to screeching across the concrete. The mourners stood in a knot out of the dog's reach and decided what to do. "That bite will get infected," Mrs. Oates assured everyone. "That poor girl could lose the nerves in her hand."

"Dr. Adenoy'll take care of her," Fred Green said, "but the dog's gone bad. It was in that motel with Buck when he died. The best thing is shoot and put it out of its misery."

Melody suggested that Mr. Burns could stuff the dog in Buck's memory.

"You'd better take it in for quarantine!" said Mrs. Oates.

But no one heard her. They went around and around about who would get to shoot Buck's dog.

Mr. Burns must have sensed the opportunity; he appeared in the doorway of Buck's bungalow with an old ranch rifle. With a rapturous gesture he lifted his rifle to his shoulder for the first time in twenty years. He fired the gun in the air and turned it on the mourners. "Git on!" he shouted. "Go home!"

That was the end of the party. Melody yelled to the boys to come in before Mr. Burns killed someone, and the mourners scattered. Some slipped around to the office first, to collect their potluck—casseroles and plates and slotted spoons among the ashes and beer cans. That was when they noticed the dark, pungent circle in Mr. Burns's chair on wheels: Mrs. Oates had wet it. In deference to Mr. Burns and the sad occasion the mourners covered their mouths to keep from laughing out loud and crept away into the blue-black evening, down the hill to town. The dog panted and whined and finally stopped barking, and soon the only noise around Mr. Burns and the Bungalows was the small rattle in the birch woods that sounds to some like the beating heart of life, and to others like just the wind.